W9-AGH-435

Lowly Behavior
Among the Upper Crust . . .

"Was she the type of woman to make enemies?"

Jane laughed. "Enemies right and left, from what I've heard. Well, perhaps enemy is too strong a word, but there were plenty of old friends who were stranded by the wayside every time Lainie Guiles took a step up. She had an eye for the main chance, that woman, and was inclined to burn her bridges. Plus—if what Donald has told me is true—she really led Hayden Lippincott on. Used him terribly, then dropped him when he hit a patch of rough sailing."

"Ah. I know the type well," replied Dewey.

"You simply *must* solve this case for us, Dewey. If you can do it in Hamilton, where everyone knows you, then it will be a snap in New York. You can ask as many questions as you like, and nobody will have a clue that you're the sleuth on the trail. They'll just think you're a nosy lady from the boondocks."

"Yes, I suppose they will—for that's what I am, you know."

"Then it's a *perfect* setup." Jane beamed brightly at her friend, who laughed.

MORE MYSTERIES FROM THE
BERKLEY PUBLISHING GROUP . . .

DEWEY JAMES MYSTERIES: America's favorite small-town sleuth! "Highly entertaining!"—*Booklist*

by Kate Morgan

A SLAY AT THE RACES   MYSTERY LOVES COMPANY
MURDER MOST FOWL   DAYS OF CRIME AND ROSES
HOME SWEET HOMICIDE

PETER BRICHTER MYSTERIES: A midwestern police detective stars in "a highly unusual, exceptionally erudite mystery series!"
—*Minneapolis Star Tribune*

by Mary Monica Pulver

KNIGHT FALL   ASHES TO ASHES
THE UNFORGIVING MINUTES   ORIGINAL SIN

TEDDY LONDON MYSTERIES: A P.I. solves mysteries with a touch of the supernatural . . .

by Robert Morgan

THE THINGS THAT ARE NOT THERE

JACK HAGEE, P.I. MYSTERIES: Classic detective fiction with "raw vitality . . . Henderson is a born storyteller." —*Armchair Detective*

by C. J. Henderson

NO FREE LUNCH

FREDDIE O'NEAL, P.I. MYSTERIES: You can bet that this appealing Reno P.I. will get her man . . . "A winner." —Linda Grant

by Catherine Dain

LAY IT ON THE LINE

SISTER FREVISSE MYSTERIES: Medieval mystery in the tradition of Ellis Peters . . .

by Margaret Frazer

THE NOVICE'S TALE

A DEWEY JAMES MYSTERY

DAYS OF CRIME AND ROSES

KATE MORGAN

B
BERKLEY BOOKS, NEW YORK

DAYS OF CRIME AND ROSES

A Berkley Book / published by arrangement with
the author

PRINTING HISTORY
Berkley edition / October 1992

All rights reserved.
Copyright © 1992 by The Berkley Publishing Group.
This book may not be reproduced in whole or in part,
by mimeograph or any other means, without permission.
For information address: The Berkley Publishing Group,
200 Madison Avenue, New York, New York 10016.

ISBN: 0-425-13471-7

A BERKLEY BOOK ® TM 757,375
Berkley Books are published by The Berkley Publishing Group,
200 Madison Avenue, New York, New York 10016.
The name ''BERKLEY'' and the ''B'' logo
are trademarks belonging to Berkley Publishing Corporation.

PRINTED IN THE UNITED STATES OF AMERICA

10 9 8 7 6 5 4 3 2 1

For Anita Raby de Gorman
And All Her Merry Brood

1

"Where to, lady?" asked the cabbie.

Dewey James settled back in the seat of the taxi. It had been many years since her last visit to New York City; but the driver's brusque manner as he growled out the time-honored question made her feel right at home.

She smiled and replied politely. "Ninety-third Street and Lexington Avenue, please."

"You want I should take the bridge? Or maybe the tunnel?"

"Oh—the bridge, by all means. Thank you."

"Right."

The cab screeched away from the air terminal, and Dewey James gazed out the window contentedly, ready for adventure. The early December day was bright, if cold; and as the driver whisked her along the airport access road, past the old World's Fair grounds, she felt a surge of happiness. It was very good to be back in New York again.

A sexagenarian widow with sparkling blue eyes and unruly silvery hair, Dewey James spent most of her days in the small town of Hamilton, seven hundred miles to the south and west of Gotham. There, by day, she plied her trade as a librarian (now semiretired) and spent her evenings in peaceful and virtuous companionship with her faithful black

Labrador retriever, Isaiah, or dining with her old friend and would-be beau, George Farnham.

For all of her small-town living, however, Dewey James knew something of the world, and she certainly knew how to enjoy herself. And, although Hamilton was a town with much to recommend it, it was not a hotbed of excitement. Thus, Dewey had been looking forward to this New York excursion with all the enthusiasm of a schoolgirl. She was coming to visit her dear friend Jane Duncan, her roommate from college days. Since their graduation, forty-some years ago, Jane's life had been a succession of exciting events that found few parallels in Dewey's quiet existence.

While the great day for her trip approached, Dewey had packed and repacked her bags, said farewell more than once to most of her friends, paid two emergency visits to Doris Bock's Tidal Wave Beauty Salon, and arranged for young Willie Grimes to look after Isaiah and her horse, Starbuck, in her absence. You might have thought she was going somewhere exotic! Well—Dewey had to admit that New York *was* exotic, even by Hamilton's standards. And Jane Duncan was, too—by any standards at all.

Now, as the taxi wove with perilous abandon through the heavy, honking traffic, Dewey hung on in the backseat, her mind racing. She grinned, remembering how Jane had looked three years ago—her tall, thin figure sheathed in a designer dress of gold lamé, her beautiful black hair, dramatically streaked with silver, swept back in a bun.

The occasion had been Jane's wedding day—more precisely, one of her wedding days: her fourth. The gentleman in the role of groom had soon proved unsavory, however, and he had shortly been given his walking papers.

Jane Duncan was a beautiful woman, rich already when she had embarked on her career of matrimonies, and richer still now by far—having been three times widowed before her divorce. Dewey didn't wonder that men longed to marry Jane—she was breathtakingly exciting. She brought herself constantly to the brink of new worlds for exploration. At every phase of her life she had found fresh passions and interests; and although she abandoned each new appetite with astonishing rapidity, the interest, while it lasted, was sincere.

In her time, Jane Duncan had been a yoga instructor and an airplane pilot; between husbands two and three (or was it one and two?), she had had a stint singing torch songs in a very exclusive nightclub. She had published her own personal fitness magazine twenty-five years ago—long before the fitness craze had taken hold. And she had, of course, been an actress—on radio and on the stage—her smooth voice somehow evoking in her audiences a deep and impassioned nostalgia, a surge of bemused longing for the sort of magical, gentle days that had never, ever existed.

Dewey roused herself from her reverie as they reached the appointed corner, and directed the cabbie to Jane's house, halfway down the block. The four-story brick townhouse looked unchanged since Dewey's very first visit to New York, forty-five years ago. The place had belonged to Jane's parents, and before them to her grandparents. Like many of the others up and down the street, it was set back slightly from the pavement; a large wrought-iron fence stood guard over a handkerchief-size garden out front.

The cabbie growled impatiently as Dewey began nervously to calculate the tip. Too much? Not enough? Impossible to know. She shrugged and handed over the money with a hopeful, apologetic air. "Here you are, then. Thank you very much."

He grunted, but his expression did not change. Feeling a little foolish, Dewey gave him a parting smile, hefted her bag out of the backseat, and mounted the familiar red granite steps.

The door was opened by a tall, handsome, redheaded man of fifty-five or sixty. He smiled a lopsided smile, full of charm.

"Ah," he said in a deep, warm voice. "You must be none other than the fabulous Dewey James."

"Oh! Yes, well, I *am* Dewey James," replied that lady, blushing with mild confusion. Her mind was still on the cabdriver, who clearly hadn't thought much of her. Some of Dewey's friends back home would have agreed that she was rather fabulous, in her own small way. But this was an opinion held chiefly by Hamiltonians. Certainly, Dewey did not think herself fabulous.

"Won't you come in?" he went on, with a courteous, proprietary air. "Jane will be down in a moment. I'm Donald Brewster." Taking Dewey's bag, he led the way into a charming front hall. Dewey followed, gazing at him with frank curiosity; he must have sensed her curiosity, for halfway to the living room he paused and turned to raise an eyebrow. Then he said, in a mischievous whisper, "I could perhaps be best described as Jane's intended."

"Ah," said Dewey, a smile lighting her face. Jane was never slow about these matters. Perhaps Dewey would be a bridesmaid yet again!

"Jane *did* tell you about me—about us, didn't she?" asked Brewster, amusement in his voice. He put down Dewey's bag near the stairs and looked at her intently.

"Er—that is—"

"I see she hasn't." Brewster chuckled and led the way into the living room. "Well, you know Jane—better than most, from what I hear. I suppose I should have let Jane tell you. But of course, I thought you knew—since you'll be here for the big day. Sit down, Mrs. James, please."

"Thank you, Mr. Brewster." Dewey looked appreciatively about her. The room was just as she remembered it from previous visits. It was full of elegant antiques, but cozy—because Jane Duncan believed that furniture should be used, not merely gazed upon. The years of long use gave the room, and indeed all the house, a feeling of history, of having seen much. She settled herself into a pretty silver-and-rose brocade sofa.

"My, my," she said, feeling at a loss for words. "That *is* exciting news. And of course, I am delighted that your big day could coincide with my visit." She smiled, wondering how much Donald Brewster knew of Jane's previous matrimonial track record.

"Yes—well, it's a spur-of-the-moment thing, actually. The wedding, that is. The proposal was well planned and perfectly timed. We're all set for next Friday afternoon, if that will suit you. Jane said you had attended her in the past, and I didn't want to break with tradition, you know." He smiled at her.

"No, heaven forfend!" replied Dewey, amusement in her voice. She had long ago stopped being astonished by anything Jane Duncan chose to do; but Jane's matrimonial antics were indeed diverting.

Donald Brewster went on. "Jane, in fact, didn't want to rush things. But since you were coming to town—well, I'm afraid I insisted. I guess you might say I owe it all to you." He smiled his handsome smile.

"My heavens!" Dewey exclaimed with a laugh.

"There is just one small hitch, Mrs. James—"

"Oh—please call me Dewey, Mr. Brewster."

"Of *course* he will," interposed an imperious voice from the hall. Jane Duncan swept magnificently into the room. She was tall and elegant, in a charcoal-gray suit with a fiery scarlet blouse; enormous pearls dangled from her ears, and at her throat was a dazzling necklace of gold. As she crossed the room to greet her old friend, the bracelets stacked along the lengths of her forearms jingled musically. "Of course he'll call you Dewey. Won't you, my darling?" She smiled at Brewster and embraced Dewey. "And you may call him Donald, or Donny—but never Don. He hates Don."

"Yes, I see," replied Dewey. "Jane—" she began.

"And *you* look absolutely wonderful, my dear," Jane interrupted. "Smashing. Superb. And how kind of you to leave your busy, *busy* life to come and see me. Your timing is perfect." She raised an eyebrow and looked at Donald Brewster. "Has my handsome Lothario let the cat out of the bag? We're tying the knot, Dewey. Isn't it too much?" She

glided over to stand next to Brewster and hooked an arm
through his. "It's all terribly hush-hush right now, until
after Thursday, for silly reasons that I shall explain later.
But we can let you in on our secret. And I hope you
approve, Dewey, I really do. It wouldn't be any good at all
if you didn't approve."

Dewey laughed aloud. It had always taken determination
to brake Jane's torrents of high spirits. Now she dived in
with enthusiasm and firmness. "I shall keep your secret for
you, Jane. Scout's honor. I want to hear all about everything."

"You shall. Run along, Donald, if you don't mind—but
first, on your way out, bring us a drink or something. We've
some catching up to do." She waved him away, and he
departed, with a wink for Dewey.

Dewey James and Jane Duncan settled in for a good,
old-fashioned chin-wag.

Not far from Jane Duncan's house, on Manhattan's Fifth
Avenue, stood a graceful limestone mansion that, for a
century, was home to the famous Bently, family, a dynasty
of American merchant-kings.

The Bentlys, alas, had all died out; but before the last
family member (Pincus Schermer Bently, IV) departed, he
had the foresight to do something for the family name,
which had been sullied by irregular profit-taking through
the centuries. Pincus Schermer Bently, IV had ensured that
the name of Bently would live on in the hearts and minds of
New Yorkers, although no Bently ever again would stroll
through Central Park or ride the IRT.

In short, Pincus Schermer Bently, IV had opted for
philanthropy.

Not that the Bentlys ever had in fact ridden the IRT or
strolled through Central Park. The family had been a
singularly sedentary group, disinclined to go anywhere at
all. It was probably their great laziness, of dinosaur propor-
tion, that had led to their eventual extinction. Their idleness

had given them a profound myopia—real and meta-physical—and had bestowed upon the last generations a chin so recessionary that it had finally disappeared altogether. It was, most assuredly, this indolent outlook that had created within the heart of every Bently who had ever breathed the desire to preserve intact the illusions of the past.

On his passing, Pincus Schermer Bently, IV, had ensured the preservation of the Bently point of view through the endowment of the Bently Foundation, which had occupied the mansion in grand style for the last twenty-five years or so. The foundation's sole purpose was to glorify a kind of life that had long ago become impossible. It had never been Pincus Bently's goal to make a contribution to the New York community; a certain amount of fame, and a good reputation, had been his aims. Yet through some perverse twist of fate his foundation had flourished, offering support to truly worthy novelists, playwrights, poets, and actors. Many of them were people whom no Bently would ever have asked home to tea.

Naturally, the Bently Foundation had swiftly become the darling charity of the very, very rich in New York. Its events and doings were faithfully recorded in the society gossip columns of three newspapers, and its staff and directors achieved a kind of popular intellectual weight that remained with them throughout their lives. "Instant *Who's Who*," someone had once remarked, when asked why she sat on the Bently board.

Four times a year the foundation opened its doors for gala dinners. There, luminaries of the theater and publishing worlds gathered to spend a thousand dollars a plate; to nod, and pat each other on the back, and generally support the work of the foundation. The Bently Mansion, open to the public on Tuesdays and to scholars by appointment, also boasted a fine small collection of early American colonial memorabilia, portraits, and maritime paintings, and an exceptional library of early American first editions. For those who liked to look back in time, the Bently Foundation was heaven on earth.

Most important of all, however, was the Bently Medallion—or, as it is more commonly known, the "Pinkie" (for Pincus Schermer Bently, IV). This prestigious prize was given each year to a writer, actor, or other artist whose work was said to exemplify the spirit of the Bently family. As might be expected, people who wrote or performed in ironic drawing-room comedies often won Pinkies; so did novelists whose tales were set among the genteel and the powerful. Occasionally the prize went to writers of nonfiction for books about the downfall of Wall Street *arrivistes*. Once (only once) it had been won by a journalist. Fortunately for New York, and for Art, the members of the Selection Committee tended to have taste as well as social standing; and the list of prizewinners was unexceptionable.

On this December morning, as Dewey James and Jane Duncan set about their chin-wagging, the Bently Foundation offices were the scene of hot and divisive debate. In the mansion's dining room four people were seated around the huge mahogany table (a wedding present from the second Pincus to his wife, Lobelia). At the head of the table was Lainie Guiles, a mousy-looking woman, bordering on anorexic, whose patina of New York sophistication didn't mask her very ordinary suburban origins. Lainie Guiles was a quick study; but her cosmetics, ambition, and mimicry of the rich and powerful could only take her so far.

The staff was having its weekly meeting—never a pretty spectacle, even when things were going well. Lainie Guiles, recently promoted to director of the Bently Foundation, had discovered that things were not going well at all. In fact, in a very short time, the operating budget for the staff was going to be running on empty, thanks to increased property taxes and a variety of other such unavoidable expenses. Lainie had recently heard from the board of trustees that the foundation would soon receive a large gift; but whether that gift would offset the terrible cash-flow problem was another question altogether.

Drastic measures were called for; in fact, drastic measures had been taken. Only the day before Lainie Guiles had dismissed Lily Feldspar, who had served faithfully for ten years as the Bently's overworked and underpaid director of community and public relations. Her going had caused much bad feeling among the small staff that remained, who suspected that the dismissal was merely a way for Lainie Guiles to consolidate her power. Lily Feldspar had been very closely identified with the Bently Foundation in the public's mind; and Terence Fenhaden, the assistant director of the Bently Foundation, felt that Lainie was up to no good.

"I want you all to understand that I had no alternative," said Lainie. "We will all have to pitch in and take on some added responsibilities as a result of this measure." She stared, glassy-eyed, at the others. "It was not a decision I am comfortable with. But there was nothing else I could do."

"Lainie, if I didn't know better, I'd swear you were on some kind of power trip." Terry Fenhaden—brown-haired, brown-eyed, with a face like a muffin, spoke with nervous contempt. He and Lainie had started out as equals at the foundation; Lainie's success had been a bitter pill for Terry. "Just because—"

"That will do, Terry," murmured Lawrence Montrose. He was a snub-nosed, dark-haired man of fifty or so, with a commanding air of self-assurance. Whether his poise came from his character or his vast fortune—the power of which delighted him—it was impossible to say. But he wielded his power with relish. Now he glared at Terry. "Let's do Lainie the courtesy of listening to what she has to say, shall we?"

Fenhaden sighed loudly. Lainie Guiles supposed she should have been grateful to Montrose for thus championing her; but she felt uneasy. Despite her crisp, professional suits and her air of efficiency, she still hadn't learned how to command respect the way Lawrence did. It was about time he relinquished control, she thought stubbornly. He was enjoying himself far too much at her expense. Lainie found herself losing her temper already—and the meeting had only just begun.

It wasn't surprising that Lawrence Montrose could command Fenhaden's respect. After all, Lainie Guiles had held the post of director of the Bently Foundation for only six weeks, but Lawrence Montrose had been the director for six years. It would take time, that was all—as Montrose had told her last night, in reassuring tones, over their second bottle of champagne at Silks.

Lainie explained the cash-flow problem to the remaining staff. They would have to cut their expenses still further. Either that, or the Pinkie Selection Committee would have to begin paying for their own dinners and theater tickets—an unthinkable alternative, as everyone knew. It would be up to the staff to pitch in and do their bit. She appealed to them, this morning, for thrift.

"It's nothing personal, Terry. Nobody's pointing a finger at you. It's a question of making ends meet." Lainie had regained her composure. She was determined not to lose her cool with Fenhaden—it was well known that he wanted her job. "We just have to cut back, that's all."

"So skip the terrapin at the Pinkie dinner Thursday night," said Fenhaden, with great logic.

Montrose raised an eyebrow.

"You know very well that's impossible," said Lainie. "Now, Marge—" She addressed herself to a dour-looking woman of forty-two or -three, with a plain face and an enormous bust. This was Marge Gantry, curator of the Bently Collection, which included not only paintings but a small library and the colonial artifacts as well. "Now— Marge. Do you have the figures for the collection's operating expenses?"

"Yes, Lainie. Right here." She tapped a folder on the table and pursed her lips. Marge was always pursing her lips, to show how serious she was about her work. To some it might have seemed an innocent habit, but it got on Lainie's nerves.

Lainie thought Marge self-important; but after all, Marge had an advanced degree in art history and a deep understanding of the foundation. Lainie Guiles was just a bit awed by Marge's knowledge and knew that the dour woman would not be easy to replace; so Lainie humored her and won her confidence by going through the motions of professional friendship. The two women were bound, by virtue of their sex, their mutual insecurity, and their shared loathing of Terry Fenhaden, in an uneasy and thoroughly hypocritical alliance. It served its purpose. Marge opened her folder and read aloud her carefully prepared, detailed memorandum, making Terry Fenhaden look bad once more.

In her small office next to the grand front door of the Bently Mansion, Maria Porter was sorting through the morning's mail. The most junior member of the Bently staff, she didn't attend the weekly meetings because she was needed to answer the telephone and do the photocopying. Maria didn't mind missing the meetings, which struck her as a boring waste of time; and this morning, as she worked, she was cheerful.

She was young, and happy in her very first real job. And a very good job it was, too—administrative assistant to the director of the Bently Foundation. All day long she took calls from celebrated writers, actors, critics, directors, and producers. They all wanted lunch with Lainie Guiles, or a word with Lawrence Montrose, or to schedule a special dinner in honor of one or the other of the rich trustees, or to meet the influential people who sat on the Pinkie Selection Committee.

Maria was not filled with grasping ambition—but still, she had hopes of a very bright future. She was clever enough to sense the opportunity before her; and she was fearless. Thus, in six short months Maria had learned to talk to the rich and famous people who telephoned, to recognize their voices, to call them "Sam" and "Herbert" and "Mimi" and even "Frank."

All of them were very nice to Maria—at first because it was politic, but later because they liked Maria. The Luminaries (as she secretly thought of them) liked her. They liked her quite a lot; and no hopeful young playwright had ever been better situated. All that remained was to persuade one or another of them to read her play.

She broke off her perusal of the morning's mail to consider, briefly, the scene in Act II that she had rewritten late last night. Her eyes, which were black as night, shone with excitement.

Today was going to be the day. Donald Brewster, author of *The Latter-Day Don Juan*, was coming by for a Selection Session with the Pinkie Committee. Donald Brewster was a very nice man; he had been quite encouraging to Maria, over the last few months.

She opened the drawer and gazed at the typescript of her play. Maria Porter was ready for him.

2

"So YOU CAN see, can't you, Dewey, that we're rather awkwardly placed. I mean to say," Jane Duncan went on, reaching for a celery stick, "that it's just the *merest* coincidence. Donald, poor lamb, is terribly impatient. But I am afraid it will look bad."

The two old friends were seated at Jane Duncan's usual table at L'Avarre, one of those tiny and elegant luncheon spots on Manhattan's Upper East Side. They were surrounded by well-kept, beautifully groomed women of a certain age, most lunching *à deux* at a leisurely pace. Dewey basked in the reflected glitter of gold and jewels from all directions, the long, well-tanned wrists of wealthy women bangled with the cheerful noise of a hundred bracelets. It was a pity, Dewey reflected, that nobody seemed to be having much fun. Nobody, that is, except herself and Jane. They had ordered extravagant lunches for themselves, chuckling over the menu with girlish glee. Now they were impatiently awaiting dessert—raspberries for Jane, a chocolate confection for Dewey. As they waited, Jane had outlined her present conundrum.

Donald Brewster, Jane had explained, had been selected as a finalist for this year's Pinkie—the Bently Medallion. Even now, as they sat finishing their lunch at L'Avarre, he was meeting with the Pinkie Selection Committee in the last stage of the arcane process (dictated by the terms of Pincus Bently's will) by which the Pinkie winner was annually chosen.

Donald Brewster's nomination for the Pinkie had come at an opportune moment in his career. His sixth play, *The Latter-Day Don Juan*, had been written after a seven-year dry spell; it had opened two months ago to very favorable reviews and was playing to packed houses in a small but upscale Off-Broadway theater. In the way of such things, the new play had stirred a revival of interest in his earlier work, and naturally he had caught the eye of the Pinkie Selection Committee; and he had been nominated for this year's Bently Medallion.

Unfortunately, this nomination had also proved awkward. By the time it was announced, Donald Brewster and Jane Duncan were an "item"—at least, privately. None of the gossip hounds had cottoned on to the fact yet, but that was only a matter of time, Jane felt. Jane, already a Bently trustee, had recently made a pledge of a million dollars to the foundation.

"If Donald wins, someone is sure to suspect unfairness," complained Jane.

"I can see that it might look odd," Dewey agreed, concentrating with an effort on Jane's problem. "What are the terms of the donation? I assume you made it anonymously?"

"Well, yes—I mean, there is of course supposed to be total secrecy as far as the *public* is concerned. But the whole Bently Foundation knows exactly where that million dollars will come from. It's not final yet—I haven't signed anything. But they need the money desperately, or so I have heard, and I would so like to give it. But, of course, the foundation is mostly peopled by—well, people one *knows* . . ." Her voice trailed off.

"Yes, yes. I do see, Jane, for all that I'm a rustic bumpkin. Now—how about the selection committee for the—the 'Pinkie,' did you call it? Are the trustees on the committee?''

"Good heavens, no. The committee is made up of critics and professors and people like that. Of course, the board is called upon to approve the selection each year, but there isn't any overlap, except for Lawrence Montrose. That man is the heart and soul of the Bently, Dewey. He seems extremely able, and one ought to be able to trust him to keep his mouth shut; but who can you trust, really? Except for you, Dewey. Which is why I so *desperately* needed you to come and see me. Shall I resign from the board? Throw Donald over? Or withdraw the gift? Tell me what to do, please. You have always been *so* wise.''

"Good gracious, Jane. I don't know. You can hardly *not* marry a man simply because he is receiving the recognition he deserves.''

"Of course not,'' Jane Duncan agreed. "On the other hand, when word gets around that we're engaged, people are just *bound* to think Donald is getting the Pinkie because of my anonymous donation.''

"Well—even if they do, Jane, he's quite successful, you know. It's not as though they had decided to give a Pinkie award to me, for example, or someone else totally out of the picture, merely to please you. Donald is an important man of letters. Why, we even have his plays in the drama section in our little library in Hamilton.'' Dewey beamed. She was justifiably proud of her library, which had been her life's work.

"Do you *really*, Dewey? Oh! He'll be thrilled, you must tell him. But—*The Latter-Day Don Juan* is not his best effort. Even Donald admits that. It has had a good run, but it was scheduled to close this week—and probably would have, if it weren't for rumors about the Pinkie. In spite of Hayden Lippincott's performance. Which has been marvelous. Extraordinary.''

"Hmm,'' said Dewey, thinking it through.

Dewey supposed it was just possible that Jane's unease

was well founded. Once the word was out about Jane's relationship with Donald, it would be only human nature to misconstrue the gift, or the award. One way and another, it did rather look like the award had been bought. The romance had certainly made things awkward.

"Let's go over it again, Jane," said Dewey, taking a small calendar from her capacious handbag. Dewey loved her handbag; but she had realized, as soon as they had taken their table at L'Avarre, that the purse was hopelessly large and out of date for this setting. It couldn't be helped, Dewey reflected. She tucked the offending satchel out of sight beneath the banquette and pointed at the calendar. "Here we are. December seventh. The awards ceremony is Thursday—that makes it the eleventh. When did you join the board?"

"Let me see . . . Well, I know it was about a month ago. About here." She pointed to a box three or four rows back on Dewey's little calendar. "I remember because I had been to see Vidor—he does my hair, you know—just the day before. An absolute magician. And he has been down with the flu, or perhaps something worse, since then. Oh, Dewey, that just doesn't bear thinking about. I can't stand for Vidor to be ill."

"Yes, I know the feeling," concurred Dewey, who had often wondered how she would cope if Doris Bock, hair-dresser to Hamilton ladies for forty-five years, should up and retire. "I know exactly what you mean. But now, let's see. You met Donald two months before that?"

"Yes—well, not to say 'met' him, really, for of course he and I had encountered each other, round about town, for many years. But he had never, shall we say, seemed so appealing before." She smiled and pointed to the calendar. "That was October. At the Zookeepers Ball, which as you probably know is a marvelous party, always."

Dewey, who knew no such thing, merely nodded.

Jane went on. "We danced the night away."

"Aha," said Dewey with a twinkle in her eye.

"We *danced*, Dewey. But then he came calling, all Edwardian and polite and everything, and invited me to take a walk with him in Central Park. An *absolute* original, that man. Well—I'll tell you. After my experience with what's-his-name—"

"Peter. Your *husband*, Jane," said Dewey, with a laugh.

"Ex. Dreadful man! Do you know, Dewey, he cheated at cards. For money. Not that he needed it. Blackguard."

"Perhaps that's how the rich stay rich, Jane," postulated Dewey.

"Not necessarily. It depends on the rich, if you follow me. Anyhow, Dewey—the thing is, Donald talked to me about the Bently Foundation, naturally. Being a playwright, he is deeply involved in the arts. *Deeply*. And of course I had *heard* of the Bently Foundation, and the Pinkie, and so forth—but Donald caused me to understand how *good* the work is that the foundation does."

"Yes—naturally," agreed Dewey. "And—if I may say so, Jane—since you were enamored of him, it was only natural for you to be interested in those things that are dearest to him."

"Well, of *course*! You see it, but then you're my friend, Dewey, and predisposed to believe in me. Heaven only knows what some of the charity-loving types in this town will think."

"But, Jane, dear—do you care what they think?" Dewey asked, reflecting that the New York which Jane Duncan inhabited really was a very small world, indeed.

"Naturally not. I don't care a fig. Except, of course, that if Donald wins the Pinkie this year, I want everyone to believe that he earned it. We're back at square one, and you haven't helped me at all, Dewey, not at all. I'm ashamed of you."

Dewey chuckled. "Jane, I think I know what you must do, in this case."

"Do you? Really, truly?" She leaned forward eagerly as

the waiter placed their desserts before them. "I *adore* raspberries. Well? Tell me, Dewey."

Dewey lifted her fork and studied the chocolate confection, her glance traveling back and forth between the mountain of dark chocolate and the utensil in her hand. Finally, she put down the fork and picked up her coffee spoon. "It's as plain as the nose on your face, Jane dear. You must merely persuade Donald that, if he wins the Pinkie, he must decline it. For the very reasons that you have mentioned to me. It won't look right, you know."

"Mmmmm," said Jane thoughtfully.

Dewey dug into her chocolate mousse.

At five-thirty the phone on Lainie Guiles's desk rang. She reached for it in a distracted manner, her eyes fixed on a report before her. "Yes? Hello?"

"I knew this world was a treacherous place, Lainie, but I really had no idea." Hayden Lippincott's voice was smooth, cool as ice, but carrying a hint of its remarkable range. He spoke softly into the telephone, leaning back easily in the deep leather sofa in his living room, and gazing out through the French doors to the terrace beyond.

"Hayden," said Lainie, unsurprised and annoyed.

"Don't sound so aggrieved, my love. I was bound to find out, you know."

"Hayden, I'm terribly busy. We've got the Pinkie on Thursday. Tell me quickly—what are you talking about?" Lainie's voice was full of irritation.

"About you and Montrose. Until I saw you together last night, I had absolutely no idea. Now it's clear as day."

"Good lord, Hayden." Lainie Guiles sighed. She made a hasty note on a pad and ruffled through a pile of computer printouts. "I haven't got time for this. And your insecurity is showing. Again."

"Actors are famous for their insecurity, my dear. Famous actors even more so. I thought you understood that."

"Hayden, he's my colleague. Besides—it's really none of your business who I see."

"Lainie."

"Anyhow," she rejoined, remembering too late to take the offensive, "what were *you* doing at Silks?"

"Celebrating, my dear. The two-month anniversary of our run."

"Well, why on earth didn't you say hello to me?"

"Oh—I didn't want to intrude. Never intrude, that's my motto. But, Lainie, really—the man is a joke."

"Good heavens. Listen, Hayden, I really have to go. I have work piled a mile high on this desk."

"I'm sure you'll have to stay late. Lawrence Montrose can be there to help you with it, fortunately."

"Hayden, you're too much," said Lainie, but not unkindly. "Goodbye." She hung up and buzzed for Maria Porter on the intercom. The eager young woman appeared in Lainie's doorway instantly.

"Yes, Lainie?"

"Maria, if Hayden Lippincott calls again, would you tell him I'm busy, please?"

"Sure, Lainie." Maria suppressed a smile. She had been watching the fireworks between Lainie Guiles and Hayden Lippincott for months now. Most women would give their right arm for a date with the most talented actor in New York; but Maria, for all her youth, knew a thing or two about love. Men weren't necessarily all they were cracked up to be. Besides—it had occurred to her that Lainie Guiles had someone new in her sights. "Anything else?"

Lainie looked up, her eyes tired. Her gaze was cool and somehow a little alien. With her too-large head above her skinny body, and her milky-eyed stare, Lainie Guiles sometimes reminded Maria of a scrawny, outsized amphibian. Much as Maria Porter wanted to like her boss, there was something decidedly creepy about her. Maria kept her distance, but politely. "Anything else?" she asked again.

"Yes. I can't find my calendar under all this mess." She gestured to her desk, its vast oaken expanse buried beneath an untidy litter of ledger books, computer printouts, unsorted correspondence, and little scrawlings on scraps of paper. "What's the name of that man who's coming by tomorrow to look at the portrait of Aaron Burr?"

"Oh—the art dealer guy. Lucas Hanover."

"Him. What time?"

"Nine-fifteen."

"Dandy," said Lainie in a tone of deep unhappiness. "That's the icing on the cake. I'm scheduled to meet with the caterers at nine. Oh, hell. Is Marge still here?"

"Of course," said Maria with a generous, cheerful laugh. Marge Gantry didn't seem to have much of a life outside the foundation. She almost never left the office earlier than eight-thirty or nine.

"Yeah—of course," echoed Lainie. "Okay. Thanks, Maria. You can go now, if you want."

"Sure. Thanks, Lainie." She smiled and bounced back out to her cubicle, scooped up her belongings, and rushed out the massive front door.

Lainie watched Maria go with affection and a twinge of envy. She, too, had once been bouncy and eager and bright—before the politics of the workplace and the venom of so many soured romances had taken their toll. Now Hayden was jealous—for no reason, really. She would have married him a year ago, six months ago. But his insecurity always seemed to get in the way; his fits of possessive anger depressed her. She was trying, for perhaps the sixth or seventh time, to make a clean break from him. But again without success.

Lainie roused herself and checked the time. Not yet six—there was plenty of time left.

On his deep leather sofa Hayden Lippincott stretched his long, elegant legs, letting the phone receiver dangle idly from his hand. He stayed that way, immobile, for quite some time, thinking about things. At last the screech of the disconnected telephone line seemed to pierce his reverie. He cradled the receiver, stood up, and glanced at his watch. Not yet six. There was still plenty of time.

3

In a cramped little office next to the gallery on the second floor of the Bently Mansion, Marge Gantry was bent over a small light table, deep in a careful examination of photographs. Next week the foundation's annual report would be sent to the printer, and she was selecting works to illustrate the brochure. Marge knew by heart every inch of the small but worthy collection that she tended, but she was a stickler for detail, deliberate in everything she did. The job would probably take her several hours, perhaps longer.

The paintings in the gallery, for the most part, were portraits and miniatures from the eighteenth century, with a few later maritime oils thrown in for size and effect. An anteroom to the gallery was lined with curio cases, filled chiefly with oddments from the military life in the Colonies. This little room was often referred to as the "sideshow"—by all but Marge Gantry, who took the sideshow in deadly earnest.

The art collection was well regarded, although it had once been much larger than it was today. Begun by the first Pincus Schermer Bently, it had increased significantly through the generations—up until the time of the Great Depression. The Bently then in residence at the great mansion had sold off a number of important items; and the last Bently had continued the process until his lawyer had advised him to hang on and wait for the prices to go up.

Marge Gantry was very good at her job—which was lucky, for she seemed to spend all of her time and energy on it. She was a tall woman, and might have been pretty if a flash of amusement had occasionally been permitted to light her eyes or relieve the creases in her brow. Unhappily, Marge Gantry was too sober for her own good. Lainie Guiles had always found Marge's company oppressive.

The Bently's director was not very wise about people; if she had been, she would have known in an instant that the problem with Marge was the chip on her shoulder, which over time had grown to boulder size. In her ten years with the foundation she had never become part of the ''scene''— never enjoyed the black-tie dinners and never left off resenting the trustees for their wealth and social prominence. Marge Gantry, in short, was a true believer, wandering in the land of the philistines.

No one at the foundation made Marge's life any easier for her, either. Terry Fenhaden was the worst—constantly riding poor Marge about her molelike devotion to her dark office and her solemn, scholastic view of her mission. But Marge had learned to cope and didn't seem to be threatened by any of the unpleasantness that often came her way—so long as it was personal. The instant, however, that there was a threat to her precious collection, she bared her fangs.

Lainie Guiles knocked at Marge's office door.

''Come in,'' said Marge, without looking up.

''Hi, Marge.'' Lainie entered and took a seat on the visitor's chair opposite Marge's desk. ''Down to the final selection?''

''Nearly. We used the other Chatard painting four years ago, but I'm not sure anyone will mind the repetition. It's appropriate, I think—the clipper ship *Ferdinand Plaisance*, in New York Harbor.'' She extended her loupe to Lainie, who peered through it obligingly at the transparency on the light table.

"Pretty. For the cover?"

"No—for the opening page to the financials in the report. I thought we'd use this for the cover—a studio shot of Lobelia Bently's wedding silver. The tea set."

Lainie looked through the loupe again. "Beautiful stuff. Too bad we can't use it to serve tea to the Selection Committee on Wednesday."

"Oh, I'm afraid that would never do," protested Marge mildly. "It's far too good for them."

"I suppose so," Lainie murmured. She took a breath. "Listen, Marge—there's something we need to talk about."

"What's that?" Marge sounded bored; her attention was once again focused on the slides before her.

"Turn that thing off, will you please?" Lainie gestured to the light box. Marge switched it off, and the gloom of the December evening welled up in the little office.

Lainie smoothed her skirt nervously and resumed. "As you will have gathered, I'm sure, from this morning's meeting, we are in a bad way. Financially. Not the foundation—but us, the staff. There's plenty of money, but there isn't really enough for the operating expenses for the coming year. And, well, Lawrence and I have been talking."

There was a flash of interest in Marge's eyes. "Talking."

"Yes. About the best way to go about getting the money we need to stay in operation. As things stand right now, I can't afford to let anyone on the staff have a raise for at least six months."

"Has anyone complained?"

"No—but that's not all. Lawrence and I have been thinking that the best way to free up the money we need is to—to—" Lainie took a deep breath. "—to see if we can scare up a buyer for one or two little things."

"A buyer!"

"Yes—well, there's been some interest, you know, from a variety of sources. There are some, er, businessmen who have expressed an interest in one or two things. Here."

"You mean sell the collection?" Marge Gantry had gone rigid, her ashen face even grayer than usual. A stray lock of hair fell across her face, and she didn't brush it away.

Lainie struggled to overcome her irritation. "Not the whole collection, Marge, for Pete's sake. Relax. Just one or two little things that will fetch us a tidy sum, keep us in business, until we are sure of things."

"Lainie, you can't be serious. What's the point of keeping the Bently Foundation in business if we cannibalize it, bit by bit?"

"Please, Marge, don't be so dramatic. It's not being cannibalized. We have hundreds of things—nobody will even notice if we sell one or two of the marine paintings."

"Nobody around here, anyway," Marge agreed sourly. "It's a stopgap measure, Lainie—a Band-Aid, that's all. When the money from selling one little thing runs out, you'll just want to sell another."

"No, no—I promise. Listen—I'll let you in on a little secret that will make this action seem more reasonable to you. Okay? Will you listen?"

Marge had set her face stubbornly; but Lainie, in the visitor's chair, effectively blocked the exit to the tiny office. Marge Gantry had no choice. She folded her arms and leaned back in her chair, all suspicion.

"It's like this," Lainie continued. "I've heard that there is a very good chance that the Bently will soon receive an anonymous endowment. A very large one."

"Rumors."

Lainie shook her head. "I don't think so. I think it's on the up-and-up. Anyhow, we'll know next week, at the latest. But in the meantime, Lucas Hanover is coming by tomorrow morning—"

"No. He's a crook and a thief, Lainie. The collection will be closed to him."

"Marge. Please. I am trying to reason with you."

"No, you're not. You are trying to bulldoze me. Terry was right—why don't you call off the caviar for the Pinkie dinner on Thursday night? That would shave a few thousand from the cost.''

"Don't be silly, Marge. You know very well that for three hundred dollars a plate we have simply got to have caviar. Besides—it's in Pincus Bently's will. As you know. The whole menu is in the will."

"Contest the will. Caviar is bad for you, anyway. Serve them bean sprouts and tofu, and to hell with them all." Marge Gantry was shaking with anger.

Lainie struggled to maintain her cool. She hated this kind of confrontation. "Marge, you know very well that we can't alienate our patrons. Without them we would be nothing at all. Be reasonable, please. I know how you feel—"

"Of course you don't, Lainie. You haven't got a clue. All you're interested in is the glitter and the rich people, and—" She broke off and looked away.

Lainie had a feeling she knew what Marge had been going to say; but she let it pass. "All right. Even if I don't know how you feel, what interests me is doing my job well. We don't really have much choice in this matter, Marge. I am asking your cooperation. If you won't show some team spirit, I will have to live with your unhappiness. But one way or another, you will see that Mr. Hanover gets everything he needs tomorrow."

"Right."

Lainie stood to go. "He'll be here at nine-fifteen, and I'll probably still be with the caterers. There's a list downstairs in my office of the things he wants to look at. We can go over it together in the morning, when you are feeling better." She tried a smile on Marge, to no effect. Small wonder—Lainie Guiles had a pathetically dim and uninspiring smile.

"And, by the way, Marge," she remarked, with a look at her watch, "the Pinkie Selectors will be here at seven, don't forget. Everyone else must be gone by the time they begin the final session."

"Oh, yeah," said Marge without enthusiasm. "For their

secret little cabal. No, don't worry, Lainie. You don't need to worry at all about me.''

Lainie Guiles departed, her sharp little heels click-clacking down the marble steps.

Marge Gantry switched on the light in the little table once more, and the office was flooded with an eerie bluish glow. Her face, illuminated suddenly from below, looked as though it had been cast in some strange, pale alloy—shiny as silver, sleek as death.

4

ON THE STAGE of the Gilman Theater, Hayden Lippincott crossed to a chair and took a seat, looking skeptically at a small book in his hands. He read aloud from the book, delivering the lines with something less than attention. The audience felt his distraction and grew restless; in the fourth row Dewey James shifted in her seat, conscious of Jane Duncan's watchful eye upon her.

It was Tuesday night. The two chums had spent the day at the Metropolitan Museum of Art, with time before and after for shopping, lunch, and tea in the Peony Room at the glorious old Marland Hotel. Dewey loved the Marland, with its legacy of old New York, the famous bar where (it was said) F. H. Lee had composed his famous limericks for the price of a drink.

They had had a quick supper with Donald Brewster at his club, the Writer's Bloc, which was not far from the Gilman Theater. Donald, with writerly reticence, had declined their invitation to attend the performance with them. Dewey reflected now that it was probably a wise decision. He had enough to be anxious about; the Pinkie Selection would be announced tomorrow.

A woman seated directly behind Dewey spoke in a noisy whisper to her companion. "Maybe he's got the flu or something."

28

"Drunk, maybe," muttered the man.

"I read he doesn't drink," the woman rejoined.

"Hush!" said Jane Duncan sharply, with a glare for the two behind them.

The Latter-Day Don Juan was really quite a fine play—full of humor and deft wordplay, with two romances, a case of mistaken identity, and a well-choreographed fight scene (with golf clubs in place of swords) for the first act closer. The play raised issues of moral importance but avoided the sin of lecturing; and if the world it depicted would soon be a thing of the past, it was nonetheless a cohesive world and accurately drawn.

Nevertheless it was clear to Dewey that the show was falling flat tonight; and the cause was undoubtedly Lippincott. Bess Carrington had performed well in the role of Lippincott's anorectic and resentful wife; and Mac Rumsen, as the buffoonish but despotic patriarch, had been full of vitality and wit.

Fortunately Hayden Lippincott, even on an off night, was magnificent in the title role. He moved like a cheetah, and managed to look woeful and wise all at once. He had a trick of lowering his voice in such a way that the audience leaned in to hear him, to be closer to him, to commune with him in his sorrows and joys. He was also enough of a professional to know when he was losing his audience and how to get them back. Tonight he threw himself with renewed vigor into the second act; and by the time the curtain fell, the play had regained its missing momentum. As Lippincott strode to the door to deliver his parting shot, he had recovered his customary intensity; and when the stage grew dark, leaving Bess Carrington alone on the spotlit set to deliver her final speech, the heart of the audience was won. There was thunderous applause as the lights went out.

Over the applause as the actors took their bows, Dewey heard the woman behind her remark, "It was all right, Alfred, but I don't think he should get a Pinkie for this one."

"Oh, I don't know, honey," her companion temporized. "Can't judge it by tonight. Lippincott was off. He was much better in *Tournament of Champions*. I still say he was drunk."

Jane Duncan raised an eyebrow inquiringly at Dewey, who smiled and patted her arm. "Don't listen to them, Jane," whispered Dewey.

"Heavens, no, I would never dream of it. I'm just *so* thankful that Donald didn't come with us. One more day before the Pinkie! It would have been too much for him, poor thing."

"You'd better hope that the Pinkie Selection Committee wasn't here tonight," remarked Dewey.

"Oh, no—they're all having their final secret session at the mansion tonight. Very medieval, the whole thing— terribly hush-hush. Their identities are supposed to be a deep secret, as well, but, of course, everyone wants to be a Pinkie Selector, so there's no change in keeping it dark if you've been tapped."

"Oh," said Dewey. "Like those secret societies at Yale or whatever."

"Worse," said Jane, "if you can imagine it. I've heard they have to put on long black robes and light the mansion with candles, or some nonsense like that. Pincus Bently was a lunatic, clearly."

"Good gracious!" said Dewey. "You mean he controls the process from beyond the grave? Oh, my." She felt a slight chill run up her spine and gathered her old woolen coat about her. Jane donned her mink, and they made their way slowly up the crowded aisle.

"The entire foundation is the legacy of a crazy old man, Dewey. Honestly, if you think I'm around the bend, you ought to hear some of the things that Pincus Bently included in the terms of the endowment. Obviously, he was a man with far too much time on his hands."

Dewey laughed. "Well, Jane, you really ought to be grateful to him, you know. He has, at least, given you a new passion in life.'' She smiled at her friend, and Jane caught the meaning of the look at once.

"I know you think me wishy-washy and frivolous, Dewey—''

"Heavens, Jane! Not at all, not at all. Just—shall we say open to suggestion?''

"Hmmm,'' replied Jane, not at all sure it was better to be ductile than frivolous.

"And enormously broad-minded, and generous, good, and kind,'' finished Dewey with a smile.

She took Jane Duncan by the arm, and they headed out of the theater.

Donald Brewster lived on Manhattan's Upper West Side, in one of those hugely elegant apartment buildings that were constructed just about the turn of the century. He had inherited the apartment, which was lucky, because none but the most successful, and commercial, of playwrights could bring home enough money to pay the maintenance on one of those twelve-room beauties today.

His living room and the master bedroom overlooked the south end of Central Park; he was accustomed, in the mornings, to rise early and go for a jog through the fresh greenery, taking in the air and the sounds of bird songs and the general peace and quiet. Brewster knew that he was spoiled by his location, but he accepted his good fortune with the same equanimity with which he greeted the failure of his fourth play, or the success of his most recent effort. It was all just a part of the ups and downs of life. He had been raised on Kipling and firmly believed in treating "those two impostors just the same.''

Early that Tuesday evening, however, Brewster's equanimity had begun to desert him. At five o'clock Andrea Follet, a professor of English and theater arts at Hencope College, had come to call. She and Donald had known each other for years, one way and another, but they had never been close friends. It was surprising that Andrea should come all the way from Hencope College—seventy blocks to the north—just to pay a social call. The reason for her visit, however, was soon clear.

"Ordinarily, Donald, I wouldn't consider even raising such an issue. After all, Shakespeare borrowed things all the time."

Brewster smiled. "Ah, but then—he was Shakespeare. Who cares where he got his stories, after all?"

"Well, yes." Andrea Follet settled herself more firmly onto Brewster's sofa—a creaking, comfortable old thing in well-worn chintz. "That's just it."

Brewster smiled at Andrea Follet. "I can see this isn't easy for you, Andrea. But go ahead—you can say whatever you like."

"All right, then." She took a deep breath. "I've got a student, a senior, who's writing a very *recherché* paper on the history of American drama. She's been doing her research in some pretty odd pockets of New York, and I have to hand it to her. So far, everything that I have checked has come out smelling like a rose."

"And?"

"And she says that *The Latter-Day Don Juan* has been lifted lock, stock, and barrel from a play called *The Runabout*, which was written in 1926 by a woman called Margaret Leslie."

"Good heavens!"

"And," Andrea Follet went on, "she hasn't got a copy of the play but knows where to find one. In other words, she can prove it."

"But I've never even *heard* of your Margaret Leslie, Andrea."

"She's not mine, Donald. She belongs to my student, who says that the only copy of the play is in the collection at the Susan Dixon Library."

"She certainly showed her scholarly mettle in going all the way to the Dixon," said Brewster. The little library, a private establishment in Midtown, was indeed an odd pocket of New York. Very few people even knew of its existence; and a trip to the Dixon, from Hencope College, was certainly venturing far afield. "Showed initiative."

"Yes. Yes, she did."

"But I wonder on what grounds she bases her allegation of plagiarism?"

"Well, her approach is kind of threefold. First of all, I should tell you that this student of mine is what you might term, for lack of a better phrase, a rabid feminist."

"Oh, dear."

"Well, it's extremely tiresome—at least, I think so. I hate having every little thing become a political issue. But that's beside the point."

"Go on, by all means." Brewster rose. "But let me fix you a drink while we talk, Andrea. What will you have? A little sherry?"

"God, no." Andrea Follet laughed. "I'm an academic, Donald, and I have been heartily sick of sherry for fourteen years. Have you any bourbon?"

"Coming right up." He opened a small cabinet tucked away in the corner, revealing a tiny refrigerator and a well-stocked bar. "Continue your tale."

"All right. Well, the feminism. You've got a line on that. In addition to which, my student is keenly ambitious. Probably the most ambitious student I've ever had."

"Out to make a name for herself?" asked Donald Brewster, pouring.

"I think so. She's rather a Young Turk. Turkesse. Turkette."

"Tur*key*?"

"Perhaps. I don't evaluate their personalities, Donald, I merely report and give them grades. She has, I think, decided that the best way to get herself accepted at the graduate school of her choice is to become famous in a hurry. Well, you can't blame her. It's an overused strategy, I think, but she's got history on her side."

"Right." Donald Brewster handed Andrea Follet her

drink and resumed his seat. He took a long pull from his own drink. An observer might have noticed that his equanimity had momentarily taken a vacation. His face was pale as ashes.

"Third thing about this young woman is a coincidence. I believe, however, that it may bear some looking into. I don't altogether trust in coincidence, do you?"

"Well, yes, actually I do. Without relying heavily on coincidence, no dramatist would ever be able to concoct a plot." He smiled, seeming restored to himself again.

"Yes, well, I didn't mean in literature. Of course we need it in literature. But in life, coincidence is odd."

"You're keeping me in suspense, Andrea."

"So I am. All right. It turns out that the forgotten dramatist Margaret Leslie was a distant relative of this young woman, which is how she knew to look her up in the first place."

"Ahh," said Donald Brewster. "Grinding the family ax."

"You could say so. Or perhaps fortune-hunting."

"Gold-digging."

"And so forth and so on." Andrea Follet smiled. "This is the reason, Donald, that I have come to you, instead of going straight to Howard Horde with the tale." She laughed, a deep, merry, bubbling laugh. Andrea Follet's dislike of Howard Horde, drama critic of the *Chronicle*, was legendary in theatrical circles. The two of them frequently squared off in public.

"Tell me, Andrea—what odds do you give your student of being right?"

Andrea Follet shrugged. "Frankly, I don't care whether or not she's right. Your play is the best thing to be produced in New York in twenty years—perhaps longer."

"And?"

"So I have given the child a grade—a good grade—for the course. But I am prepared to do battle with her, if you think the situation merits it."

* * *

In the darkened, drafty dining room of the Bently Mansion, spectral shadows danced on the ancient wallpaper. The antique chandelier above the table glittered with the light of a hundred small candles; the wall sconces, similarly outfitted, shone with a romantic radiance. On the table were four very valuable hurricane lamps, casting a diffuse, even glow on two bottles of vintage port (both nearly empty) and five small crystal glasses. On a silver tray (eighteenth-century American, very rare) were the leavings of two large rounds of cheese; the tablecloth was littered with the crumbs of countless crackers.

Around the table were gathered the five chosen ones—the Bently Medallion Selection Committee, whose task it was to make their final determination in awarding this year's Pinkie.

By the rules of Pincus Bently's strange bequest, the Selectors were required to wear long black gowns, trimmed with ermine, for the ritual known as Last Night; even in this dim light, the fur on the robes looked a trifle moth-eaten. It was now nearly eleven-thirty, and after four hours of hot debate the people wearing the robes also looked a little the worse for wear.

The Selectors had eliminated Ferris Fournier's book, *Secret Dreams*, as being too racy for a Pinkie (although the novel had claimed three other prizes of distinction within the last eight months). Similarly, they had erased from the slate the new robotic ballet, *Jerk*, by Susan Van Allan; and the latest collection of poetry by Harry Cryer. By ten-fifteen the choices had been whittled down to two: Donald Brewster, for *The Latter-Day Don Juan*, and Alexander Mercer, for his comic novel *Silver Spoons and Darning Needles*. But on these two lemmas the committee had foundered.

Sophia Fuller, chief of the Old New-York Historical League, yawned and glared at Peter Rommel, president and publisher of Wayward Press. Rommel stubbornly refused to get into the spirit of the thing—to make his choice and let everyone go home. He was afraid that casting his vote for any one person might alienate the losers. Rommel had dined out rather elegantly indeed over the months since the nominations had been made. There might be lucrative book contracts at stake; and he certainly didn't want to circumscribe his party circuit.

Howard Horde, chief literary critic of the *Chronicle*, puffed on a cigar and leaned back, exhausted, in his chair. His gray cheeks sagged a bit, and his nose was rather red; but despite his corpulence and his lassitude, he was known about town as one sharp operator. Horde raised an eyebrow at Andrea Follet. Andrea Follet raised a retaliating eyebrow back at Horde. She despised his criticism.

Lawrence Montrose sat at the head of the table, sunk in gloom. He looked at his watch and reached for the near bottle of port.

"Well, Larry?" asked Horde, at last breaking the dreary silence. "It's up to you, you know."

"Not until Rommel casts a vote. Sorry," said Montrose, and looked it.

"Come *on*, Peter," insisted Sophia Fuller.

Rommel ran a hand through his bushy gray hair, then rubbed his face in his hands. "I can't help it, you know. I just don't like having to choose between two friends."

"If you don't like choosing, you shouldn't have joined the Selectors," pointed out Andrea Follet, reasonably and agreeably. "But, since you're here, Peter, and we're here with you until you make up your mind, I think—"

"She's right," interrupted Horde. "Great Scott, man. They should never have let you join this committee."

"But, Howard, I didn't know then that I was going to have to vote against one of my friends."

"Look in that rule book again," said Sophia to Montrose. "Are you sure he can't abstain?"

"For God's sake, Peter," said Montrose bitterly. "This is not the UN Security Council. It's just a prize. Tell you what." He leaned forward. "I'll make sure that whoever loses finds out how hard this was for you. Will that suit you?''

"I suppose so," said Rommel glumly.

"All right, then. Are we ready to proceed?"

Four heads nodded in agreement.

"Very well, then. We proceed. I wish this part weren't so foolish, but I guess it can't be helped. Pincus Bently was a very foolish man." Lawrence Montrose stood up and began to speak in Latin. *"Arma virumque cano."*

When it came time to utter the Incantation, Montrose always felt idiotic. Someone had once told him that the lines in Latin came from Virgil's *Aenead*, but the words held no significance for him other than as a part of this archaic little ceremony. Something about singing, he thought it was, and maybe something about virility. He wasn't sure. But as he looked around the room, he could tell that he wasn't alone in his ignorance.

He sat down again, and Horde stood. *"Troiae qui primus ab oris Italiam fato profugus Lavinaque venit litora."*

Andrea Follet stood. *"Multum ille et terris iactatus et alto vi superum,"* she recited.

"Hic, haec, hoc," muttered Rommel from his chair, waving a large hand. "Can't remember it."

"Nice move, Peter," commented Horde. "What do you do all day in that office of yours? Surely you don't read."

"Saevae memorem Iunonis ob iram," finished Sophia Fuller, in a tone of relief. As the newest Selector, Sophia wasn't really supposed to speak the Incantation; but Montrose overlooked the infringement.

"All right, then. So much for Virgil—thank you, Sophia." Montrose glared at Rommel. Next year Rommel was out. Without a doubt.

Now the robed figures began to move about the room, extinguishing the candles in their sconces. With a long-handled snuffer Lawrence Montrose put out the lights in the chandelier. Finally they returned to the table, and Andrea

Follet blew out the candles under the hurricane shades. The room was in total darkness, and silence descended.

At last Montrose spoke. "Number one?"

Howard Horde spoke. "For the Bently of the Year, I choose Brewster, with good cheer."

"Number two?"

Andrea Follet repeated the sentence. She was followed by Peter Rommel, and finally by Sophia Fuller.

Montrose spoke again. "Yea, I say, that this bequest/ Shall go to no one but the best." He pounded a small gavel, stood, and sighed. "All done. Finished. Andrea, see if you can find the light switch over there, would you?"

There was a scraping noise as Andrea Follet rose from her chair; she fumbled for the light switch, and suddenly the room was harshly illuminated, throwing into stark relief the shabbiness of the gowns, the mess of crumbs on the table, and the glasses, stained about their rims with a crust of bloodred port.

"Thank you all, very much," said Montrose. "Pincus Bently would be proud, very proud indeed."

Outside of the Bently Mansion, Howard Horde and Lawrence Montrose stood in a pool of light. Horde was still puffing on the stump of his cigar; Montrose had lit a malodorous and very expensive Turkish cigarette. The wind had come up, and the two men turned their collars up against the cold.

"How about a real drink somewhere, Larry?" asked Horde. "Get rid of the taste of that god-awful port. What about it? Think Brewster will play in Peoria?"

"That's vintage port, Howard," said Montrose, ducking the question. "But I suppose all those years of swilling cheap bourbon have dulled your palate."

"Bourbon works for me. How about it?"

Montrose glanced at his watch. Midnight. "No, not tonight. I have to be at the foundation early tomorrow to tell Lainie about the decision."

"Let's call her now."

"No."

"What the hell, man? She's kind of cute, I think."

"Huh."

"You don't think so? I thought you two were kind of an item." Horde scrutinized Montrose's face.

"That's what she'd like everyone to think, Howard."

"Gotcha." Horde looked at his watch, puffed heavily on his cigar, and tightened the scarf around his throat. "No point in freezing to death. See you, Montrose."

"Right."

Howard Horde wandered rather unsteadily down the street; Lawrence Montrose, oblivious to the cold edge of the wind, stood looking after him until he turned the corner. Then he made an about-face and reentered the Bently Mansion. He had left something behind.

5

"I'M *REALLY* SORRY, Mr. Hanover," said Maria Porter for the fourth or fifth time in less than half an hour. "She really should have been here. She didn't forget about you, honest. Something must have come up."

Lucas Hanover shifted comfortably in the large leather armchair in the foyer of the Bently Mansion and smiled up agreeably at Maria. A swarthy man in his late thirties, with dark hair and lively brown eyes, he radiated success and aesthetic elegance. He glanced at his watch—an antique Patek Phillipe—and shrugged slightly. It was nine-forty-five; Lainie Guiles was half an hour late. "I don't mind waiting another five minutes or so, Maria," Hanover remarked equably. "I always bring my work with me, you know." He nodded to indicate the sleek leather portfolio in his lap; he had spent the last few minutes making notes in it with a beautiful fountain pen. Maria suspected that the portfolio contained nothing but a list of very rich people, with annotations about how much cash they might be likely to drop for the sake of Art to hang on their walls. That was all right. She approved of Hanover as a man who could persuade people to part with money for things that were actually worth something.

Lucas Hanover was one of the city's most prosperous fine-art dealers. He had begun life with many advantages, it was true; but he was deeply knowledgeable and had worked very hard to attain his position of preeminence in the New York art world. The key to his success had more to do with psychology than anything else; his ability to match an expensive painting with a well-heeled buyer was little short of miraculous. The upper crust sought him out for advice and sage counsel as though he were a doctor, or a priest, or even a hairdresser.

"Okay," said Maria. "Do you want some coffee or something?"

"No, thank you." He picked up his pen and began again to write.

A moment later the front door opened to admit Terry Fenhaden, arriving to work a little earlier than his customary time of ten o'clock. He looked at Hanover, surprise on his muffinlike face. He squared his rounded little shoulders as much as he could square them and approached Hanover with hearty familiarity.

"Lucas!" he exclaimed, his voice warm with the pleasure of being on first-name terms with a person of Hanover's importance.

Hanover hid his distaste; he was naturally courteous and usually found that it didn't hurt to be polite. "Hello, Terry," he replied, cordially but without warmth.

"Good to see you, good to see you. Why didn't you tell me you'd be by this morning? Maria, get Mr. Hanover some coffee, like a good girl."

Maria suppressed her irritation and started for the kitchen, but Hanover stopped her with a smile. "No, honestly Maria, I'm fine." He turned to Fenhaden. "Actually, Terry, I was just on my way out. Only came in to see Lainie and Marge, but apparently we've all got our signals crossed."

"Marge. Marge *Gantry*?"

"Yes. Marge, however, is down with the flu, according to my friend here." He nodded toward Maria.

Fenhaden glowered at Maria. "Then why did you keep Mr. Hanover waiting, Maria, if Marge is sick?"

"Because Lainie was supposed to be here soon, Terry," Maria responded with spirit. "She must have gotten hung up with the caterers."

"Well, then for godsake call the caterers and find her." He shook his head and looked at Hanover, man to man. Hanover, however, refused to play. It was evident that he liked Maria Porter.

"Maria has been most kind and helpful, Terry. And she *has* called the caterers. There was no answer." He pulled on a beautiful cashmere overcoat and wrapped a colorful silk scarf about his throat. "Thank you so very much, Maria. I'll be off. Make my excuses to Lainie, will you?"

"Sure thing, Mr. Hanover," replied Maria with a grin.

"And Maria—call me Lucas." He winked at her and departed.

Terry Fenhaden, usually rather an unpleasant young man, was in a foul temper this morning. He wheeled on Maria. "Nice going."

Maria ignored him and returned to her office, where she tried again to track down Lainie Guiles. No luck. Maria looked at her watch—ten-fifteen. She was beginning to worry.

Half an hour later Lawrence Montrose appeared. On his heels was Madeline Hoffman, whose firm was catering the Pinkie dinner. She was a small, elegant woman, blond and blue-eyed, with a cheerful, busy air. Maria watched in silence as Montrose stuck his head into Lainie's office. "Not here?"

"No," said Maria. "I thought she was with Mrs. Hoffman." Maria looked inquiringly at the woman.

"No, she didn't come by, and I had to rush down to Petrossian to check on the caviar order, and thought I'd pop in on my way back."

Terry Fenhaden popped out of his office. He hated to miss out on anything. "Oh, hello, Madeline. You haven't got Lainie, have you?"

"No, I haven't, I'm sorry to say. Terry, I don't suppose *you* know anything about the place settings?"

"Ah—sorry, Madeline. Check with Lainie when she turns up. Not my kind of thing."

"No," agreed Madeline Hoffman. She had been catering the Pinkie dinner for five years; never once in that time had Terry Fenhaden been able to muster the enthusiasm to help out. "Well, ask her to call me, will you?" Madeline Hoffman departed.

"Listen, Lawrence," said Fenhaden in a low voice, when Madeline Hoffman had gone, "have a word with Maria, won't you? We have got to have some order around this place. Lucas Hanover was kept waiting here for nearly an hour this morning."

Montrose, taking off his overcoat and hanging it over the back of the banister, smiled. "Is that right, Terry?" He turned to Maria, but Fenhaden cut in again to explain, making clear his annoyance with Marge for being sick, with Lainie for her truancy, and with Maria just for being there. Lawrence Montrose listened in silence, leaning up elegantly against the newel post. Maria reflected, not for the first time, that Terry Fenhaden was a true and utter pill.

"Oh, well, Terry," said Montrose, when Fenhaden's spate was through. "I don't suppose Lucas minded. We're doing him a favor, you know."

Montrose walked into Lainie's office and picked up the phone. He dialed, listened, and then hung up.

"Maria," he called.

"Yes, sir?"

"Have a look." He spun Lainie's desk calendar around. "She's got appointments stacked up all day. You sure you haven't heard anything from her?"

"Nope. Not a word," Maria called back. Montrose began to pace in the elegantly proportioned room. He finally seemed to come to a decision; he stopped pacing and made his way to Maria's desk.

"She's probably over at the Palmer House," said Montrose. "Checking up on things."

Fenhaden, who had been hovering just outside the door to his own office, protested. "If she's there, she'll be along soon."

Montrose looked at him abstractedly. "Terry, maybe you should run over there and see if you can find her."

"Why don't we just call?"

"It's only around the corner, Fenhaden."

"What on earth for?"

"You need the exercise." Montrose poked at Fenhaden's flabby belly. "You look terrible. Too young to be fat." Lawrence Montrose was one of those tall men blessed with a lean, athletic frame. He would never know the frustrations of trying to shed a few inches from his girth; and with an impatience typical of many people upon whom Nature has smiled in this way, he didn't understand what all the fuss was about.

Terry Fenhaden, sensitive about his weight, gave Montrose a look of utter loathing. Without further protest, however, he donned his coat and departed, and Montrose sat down at Lainie's desk to wait, a self-satisfied look upon his handsome features.

Maria settled back to her work. "People sure are *weird*," she muttered to herself. "Bizarro."

Before long there was another intrusion into this already chaotic day at the Bently. The front door opened to admit Jane Duncan, with Dewey James in tow.

"Hello, Jane," said Montrose in a cheerful tone as the two ladies came into view. "Come in, come in."

Jane Duncan swept into the foyer, magnificent in mink. "Hello, Lawrence," said Jane warmly. "I don't know if you've ever met my dearest friend, Dewey James? We roomed together in college, you know. Dewey, meet Lawrence Montrose, the absolute heart and soul of the Bently. It was Lawrence," she added in an undertone, "who talked me into parting with my money."

They exchanged greetings, and Jane Duncan went on. "Lawrence, Dewey and I have just poked our noses in for the fun of it today. I know everyone must have a hundred things to do, with the Pinkie dinner tonight and everything, but I did so want Dewey to have a nice look around. I've bored her to tears already with talk of nothing but our good works here. And I wanted to tell Lainie that Dewey will be coming as my guest to the dinner tonight. If there's room, of course."

"Marvelous. Very pleased to have you here, Mrs. James." He bowed, polite but dismissive. "We're a little short-handed today, but perhaps Maria can at least show you around quickly upstairs." He called to Maria, who joined them and was introduced to Dewey James. "Take Mrs. James upstairs, will you, Maria?" he said sharply. "But before you go," he said, grabbing her by the elbow, "tell me. Where the *hell* is Lainie?"

"*Here* is Lainie," said a voice from the hall. The front door shut with a loud bang, and Lainie Guiles blew into the foyer, bringing with her a gust of cold December air. Everyone turned around, and Montrose took three angry strides toward her.

"Where have you been? We've been worried sick about you."

Lainie Guiles gave Montrose a long stare, amusement playing over her thin lips. She was a small woman, thin almost to the point of anorexia, with curly brown hair and a small-featured, somehow stingy-looking face. Dewey noticed at once the glassy-eyed complacency with which she met Montrose's wrath; she gave the impression of feeling that interpersonal contact was too great an effort to bother with. Dewey wondered idly what on earth Hayden Lippincott, who radiated warmth and passion from the stage, could find to like in this tepid woman. "I had some things to do, Lawrence," Lainie Guiles went on. "What's the matter with you?"

"The matter is that this place is in an uproar, Lainie. The

caterer was here looking for you, and Lucas Hanover came and went. I just sent Terry Fenhaden over to the Palmer House to see if he could find you. Marge is out with the flu. And, in case you've forgotten, the Pinkie Dinner is scheduled for six o'clock this evening.''

"Cool your jets, Lawrence.'' Lainie unwound a fine, plum-colored cashmere scarf from her neck and tossed her mink coat casually onto the hall chair where Lucas Hanover had waited for her. "Everything is under control. I suggest you go home and work on your speech.'' She passed into her office and shut the door behind her.

Maria Porter gave Dewey a smile. "I'll let Lainie know that you'll be at the dinner tonight. But maybe we should postpone that tour, Mrs. James?''

"Absolutely,'' agreed Dewey with a vigorous nod. "Another day will do, Maria. Thank you.''

Maria laughed gently and headed for Lainie's office. Dewey and Jane glanced toward Montrose. Then, with a common purpose, they gathered their coats firmly about them and headed for the front door.

"Whew!'' said Jane when they were once more on the sidewalk.

"Goodness!'' agreed Dewey. "Quite a hubbub.''

"Everyone is nervous about the dinner tonight, I suppose. Let the chips fall where they may, Dewey—I just hadn't the heart to ask Donald to decline the Pinkie. Who cares if people talk?''

"Who cares,'' agreed Dewey, glad that Jane was over her conflict-of-interest crisis. Some fresh topic had probably surfaced to worry about.

"Anyway,'' said Dewey, "it's rather a big deal. The mayor will be there. *And* the head of the Public Library, and the director of funding for the state arts foundation. Not to mention the ubiquitous press, including Lisa Hughes, who does the society page gossip for the *Chronicle*.''

"An impressive lineup, no doubt,'' replied Dewey as they turned left and headed north along Madison Avenue.

"I suppose. You never know, do you, when you're going to need someone's help. In New York it's a good idea to have everyone on your side—because if they're not for you, they're against you. Lawrence Montrose is very good at making sure they're for him."

"Yes, I imagine he is. Funny—I sense that he and Lainie don't care for each other very much."

"Now, what on earth gave you that idea, Dewey?" replied Jane with an enigmatic smile. "If I had to bet, I'd bet that Lawrence Montrose is teetering on the brink."

"Oh," said Dewey, considering. "Yes, perhaps you're right."

"Which means that dear old Hayden Lippincott may soon find himself out in the cold. And speaking of the cold"—Jane gathered her coat closer about her—"I'm freezing. What do you say we take a cab home?"

"What a lovely idea," said Dewey.

6

DONALD BREWSTER, RESPLENDENT in a white dinner jacket, was the *beau idéal* of a Bently Medallion recipient. Tall and handsome, with enough old-fashioned elegance to outfit the *Queen Mary*, he had the knack of listening to everyone who talked to him, and of remembering not only their names, but also what they talked about. This aptitude had helped him greatly in his career as a playwright; he had, along with his memory, a keen ear for the way people talked at each other, and over each other, and around each other. These habits of conversation found faithful expression in his plays, which despite their rather *recherché* settings—among the handful of families who still found themselves in possession of Old Money, and all the neuroses that went with it—had a universal appeal that owed much to Brewster's remarkable ear for thoughts that went unspoken but not unexpressed.

The Bently Dinner was held (as it was every year) at the old J. Preston Palmer House on Sixty-ninth Street, not far from Fifth Avenue. The house, which was now an elegant gentlemen's club, was as perfect a setting for a Bently Dinner as it would be possible to imagine. The place was really more of a museum than a club; like the Bently Mansion, it had been frozen in time at about the year 1908. The interior was lavish but not showy, with fine marble floors and the floor-to-ceiling windows and doors that

48

seemed to Dewey James, quietly sipping Dubonnet in a corner, to be more the rule than the exception in New York mansions. The quiet, soft-footed servants who came and went, with trays of hors d'oeuvres and bottles of champagne, seemed to Dewey to belong to another place and time. She took it all in cheerily, never for a moment wishing that her own little Hamilton Ladies Lunch Club could be like this—but happy that such things still existed, in odd pockets of the world like Manhattan. She couldn't wait to get back home to Hamilton and tell her friend, George Farnham, about the way they did things at the J. Preston Palmer House.

Dewey woke from her absorption to see Maria Porter approaching, radiant in a dress of bright scarlet silk, with a beautiful pearl necklace about her throat and a handsome young man, with merry-looking, hooded eyes, on her arm. "Hiya, Mrs. James," said Maria, her dark brown eyes sparkling brightly. "Isn't this fun? Mrs. James, this is Danny Parker."

Dewey shook hands with Maria's friend. "It most certainly *is* fun, Maria. Are you having a good time?"

"You betcha. You'll never believe this, but I just talked to that guy over there"—she nodded discreetly—"the round guy, with the glasses. See him? In the polka-dot tie."

"Yes, I do see him. Who is he?"

"His name is Eric Brody. He works for the New American Playwrights Festival, and guess what? He said I could send him my *play* to read." Maria beamed, and Danny Parker beamed along with her.

"Isn't *that* wonderful?" Dewey was really pleased. She found Maria Porter utterly charming and wondered now, not for the first time, how a young woman in pursuit of fame and fortune in New York managed to stay so wholesome.

"Not that he'll like it, necessarily," Maria added with perfect candor. "It's a little too square for the Festival crowd, I think. But at least if he doesn't, I can maybe ask him for the names of some other people who will."

"Very smart of you," said Dewey. "But I'm sure he will like it, and then you'll be the toast of the town, this time next year."

"That's right, Mrs. James," concurred Danny.

"Yeah, right," replied Maria, grinning broadly nonetheless. "Well, still, I guess you never know. Look at somebody like Madonna. Out of nowhere."

"I'd rather *not* look at Madonna, thank you just the same," responded Dewey with a laugh.

"I know what you mean. But this is definitely a hotbed, this place."

"Is it, now? Tell me about some of the other guests, you two. Are they all famous people?"

Maria nodded. "Mostly. Well—famous in New York, anyway. Some of them, like that guy over there with the stains on the front of his jacket, are just kind of famous for being famous." Dewey turned and saw a fat, balding man with greasy glasses and a large brown spot on the lapel of his white dinner jacket. Maria went on. "His name is Garrett Brown. He's a writer. He likes to hobnob a lot and gets good magazine assignments because everybody thinks he knows the inside scoop on everyone else. Nice racket. Danny knows him." She elbowed Danny playfully, and he laughed.

"I don't actually *know* him," he protested. "But he wrote a pretty nasty piece about my father's law firm in the *Clarion Call*."

"We don't like him," Maria clarified. "In fact, we sort of hate him."

"Hmm," said Dewey, studying Garrett Brown. She wondered how he managed to put it over on people so consistently, if even young Maria Porter was on to his tricks. Maria read Dewey's mind. "I hear he's very good at keeping secrets."

"Ah."

Danny Parker grimaced. "At keeping them until he's ready to use them."

"Right," Maria agreed. "Now, the guy over there, with the bright blue tie on," Maria went on, "is Lucas Hanover. He's an art dealer. He's really nice."

"Is he, now?"

"Yeah. He came to see Lainie and Marge this morning and didn't even get mad when they didn't show up."

"No?"

"Nah. He says he can always keep himself occupied. Terry Fenhaden adores him and wishes he could be like him; but Mr. Hanover hates Terry. Well, practically everybody hates Terry," added Maria in a near-whisper. "But that's because he always hates them first."

"I see," said Dewey, unsure of whether Maria hated Terry or not. On the whole, she thought probably not; Maria didn't seem the type to fall into that kind of trap. Also, Terry Fenhaden was easily ten years her senior, and she really was Lainie's personal assistant, not hired help for the whole foundation. Thus Terry Fenhaden was probably too far removed from Maria, on a day to day basis, for her to be bothered by him. "Which one is he?" she asked.

Maria looked around at the assembled guests. Eventually she spotted Fenhaden, who was off in the farthest corner, deep in conversation with a beautiful young woman. "Over against the fireplace wall," reported Maria discreetly. "The one with a kind of pushed-in face, dark hair, and a mustache."

"Talking to the blond woman?"

"Right. I don't know who that is. Probably his date."

"And what about Marge Gantry? Did she get over her flu in time to attend?"

Maria looked around the room again. "She hates parties anyway, so if she was still feeling sick, there's no way she'd turn up. No—wait. I see her. She's over near the bar, talking to Mr. Hanover."

Dewey scanned the room until she caught sight of the gleaming good looks of Lucas Hanover; the woman talking to him was tall, with dull brownish hair and a serious expression in her eye. There was a deep red flush on her cheeks, which from this distance gave her the appearance of having put on two bright spots of rouge. "She looks as though she's having an extremely serious conversation," Dewey remarked.

"She always looks that way," replied Maria, glancing over her shoulder toward Marge and Hanover. "That's just the way she looks. But her face is all red. Probably still has the flu."

"Indeed. It was good of her to attend the dinner, in that case," said Dewey, a trace of irony in her voice.

Across the room, unaware of the scrutiny she bore, Marge Gantry was bringing her conversation with Lucas Hanover to a close.

"I don't understand, Lucas," she said, now for the third or fourth time. "The collection is not for sale. Not any part of it. And *certainly* not our Edmé Chatard."

Hanover smiled and crossed his arms, his brown eyes radiating charm and warm fellow-feeling. He spoke as one art lover to another. "I know how you must feel about this, Marge. But believe me, nobody will know. Nobody. My buyer—"

"I don't, frankly, give a damn about your buyer, Lucas." The red glow on Marge Gantry's cheeks intensified, and she spoke hoarsely but with deadly earnestness. "I am responsible for that collection. There will be no sale."

"*Au contraire*, my friend," replied Hanover, his good humor not at all perturbed by Marge's outburst. "There has already *been* a sale."

"No."

"You mean you really don't know about this, Marge?"

Marge Gantry looked stubbornly, warily at Hanover, but she didn't reply. Hanover reached over and took one of her large, weatherbeaten hands. "Marge—I can't help it if that place operates like a snake pit. I had no idea that you would oppose the deal—nobody told me. Nobody told me that you hadn't even been informed."

"Hah."

"Honest. Listen—would I do that kind of thing to you?"

"How do *I* know, Lucas? Probably, if the price was right. Everyone's got a price, Lucas."

"All right, you go right ahead and think that way, if it will make you feel better."

"I'll block the sale."

Hanover shook his head. "Too late. It's a done deal. I've got the painting—picked it up today. All that remains is for my buyer to take possession."

Marge Gantry's face was a study in pain and betrayal.

"Hey—it'll be good for the Bently. I promise. Big cash flow."

"She had *no right* to do that behind my back," said Marge Gantry bitterly. "None. No right at all. I'll take her to court."

"Come off it, Marge. Don't let her get to you. Besides, I'm sure you'll feel better if I tell you who the buyer is. In the strictest confidence, of course. The trustees have sworn me to secrecy, but I think, after all, that you deserve to know."

"To hell with you, Lucas Hanover," said Marge in a quiet voice. "To hell with you." She turned on her heel and stormed away.

"Touchy little thing, isn't she?" remarked a smooth voice behind Hanover. He turned to see Terry Fenhaden, a look of smug satisfaction on his face. It was impossible for Lucas to know how much of the conversation Fenhaden had overheard.

"Go play in traffic, Terry," was Hanover's cheerfully dismissive reply. He polished off his drink in one quick gulp and headed to the bar for a refill.

At seven o'clock the dinner was served according to the dictates of the will of Pincus Schermer Bently, IV. This meant, for the fastidiously health-conscious diners of the 1990s, a choice between their consciences and the certain knowledge that this would be a meal to write home about. All but the most tiresomely abstemious prepared gleefully for an evening of indulgence.

Because Dewey James had been a last-minute guest, Lainie Guiles had placed her at the table reserved for the Bently Medallion Selection Committee—which happened to be the only table with a free spot. Not that Dewey would know that she was sitting with the Selectors; their identities were supposed to be a secret. In practice, the secret was rather an open one, but everyone did his best to keep up the charade. And Dewey, of course, had no idea. Still, as she took her seat, she had the sensation of breaking a very strict rule, of committing a transgression for which everyone involved was secretly glad.

As Dewey tucked in with relish to the first course— Chincoteague oysters—she did her best not to feel out of place; but she needn't have worried. The Selectors had spent one evening a week, for the last three months, in each other's company; as the natural result of such prolonged exposure, they were heartily tired of one another and reasonably glad of a new face, however unexciting or unglamorous.

On Dewey's left was Peter Rommel, the rubicund publisher of the Wayward Press, to whom the Pinkie selection had caused such great agony, because he had been forced to choose between two friends. On her right was Howard Horde, the gray-cheeked drama critic of the *Chronicle*. He had made quite a business, as he sat down, of extinguishing his fat cigar; Dewey was thankful for small favors. Opposite Horde was Lawrence Montrose, who gave no sign of ever having seen Dewey before. She let it pass; this was a big evening for the Bently Foundation, and really, her presence here was probably an outright intrusion.

Both Horde and Rommel had said hello, and inquired politely how Dewey was, and listened with deepening abstraction as she meekly related the reason for her presence. Over the oysters, as Dewey mentioned her little library in Hamilton, Howard Horde dropped all pretense of politeness and began to talk loudly to Lawrence Montrose about the plans for a new incinerator on the East River, opposite Sutton Place. Dewey was surprised but not hurt; she knew that New Yorkers could be very provincial. Rommel kept up a conversation with her in fits and starts, but he gave up entirely when Dewey began to ask him about the business of publishing. She could tell, from the supercilious look that flitted across his face, that he expected the worst from her. He was probably worried that she might ask him to publish her novel, or—worse—her memoirs. She let it pass and ate her supper in silence for a time, listening with only half an ear to the talk of incinerators.

The oysters were followed by diamondback terrapin, served from huge tureens of antique French silver. As a silent-footed waiter placed a soup bowl before Dewey, she realized, with grim apprehension, that they had only reached the "fish course." She had never in her life seen such an elaborately produced meal. Jane Duncan had told her that the menu was established by Pincus Schermer Bently, IV, and that no deviations from the set meal were permitted. Dewey wasn't sure she would survive the onslaught of such rich food, especially if it had to be consumed in the conversational void occasioned by the bad manners and snobbery of Howard Horde and Peter Rommel.

Fortunately the evening was saved for her by the two female members of the Selection Committee, Andrea Follet and Sophia Fuller. Over the Cornish game hens they smiled at her and made a few quiet remarks; by the time the roast beef arrived, they had taken pity on her. Both women had suffered through enough endless meetings with Horde and Rommel to know what boors they could be. Andrea Follet, with a look of mischief in her eye, began to regale Dewey with stories of prior Bently Medallion winners, and tales of the deep oddness of the Bently family in general.

Sophia Fuller, as head of the Old New-York Historical League, was a fountain of information about the family; not just the New York Bentlys but other relatives scattered across the East Coast. From time to time, Sophia told Dewey, she received letters of inquiry from far-flung Bentlys—usually when their own means were running short. Sophia Fuller usually responded with letters full of polite references to legitimacy as the basis of inheritance law. She found that this approach had many merits.

Andrea Follet was deeply amusing on the subject of the latest production at the Experimental Stage in Brooklyn. The entertainment in question, entitled *The Heisenberg Principle*, was billed as something called an *opéra naturel*; it involved a series of single notes blown on a bassoon, with a pair of chimpanzees, upstage, beating on a drum at intervals. This effort had won vast acclaim, not least from the *Chronicle*. Andrea Follet's infectious laughter on the subject eventually inflamed Howard Horde, who had written a long, flowery, and thoroughly positive review on the show, full of references to Einstein, Pascal, Leibniz, and Teilhard De Chardin.

In the midst of the salad course (which Dewey heartily hoped would be the *last* course of this seemingly endless meal), Horde pounded his fist on the table, causing everyone's wineglasses to jump. He snarled and let forth with a diatribe against women in academia and a general dismissal of Hencope College, where Follet was a tenured professor, as a breeding ground for unhealthy appetites and radical feminism. Andrea Follet responded with mirthful retorts and more laughter, which only made Horde angrier still.

When the salad plates were cleared away (Dewey, with a quick glance at her watch, realized that they had been eating steadily for nearly two hours), Lawrence Montrose stood and cleared his throat. As dessert was served (with the Château d'Yquem), he made a quick and polite little speech about the merits of *The Latter-Day Don Juan*. Then Donald Brewster rose to speak in eloquent and moving tones about the importance of foundations to the work of struggling artists. Dewey, with a fleeting thought for Jane Duncan's millions, suppressed a chuckle. Brewster thanked everyone, most especially the Selectors, and of course (here he took Jane's hand), the support of his loving and generous friends.

There was a spattering of applause, and then a long silence.

"Here we go," said Andrea Follet to Dewey. "Just when you thought you might escape back to the twentieth century."

Sophia Fuller raised her eyebrows and smirked. "The ladies now withdraw to the upstairs withdrawing room."

"If you can believe it," appended Andrea. "Be grateful for small favors, though. If this were Rhodesia in the colonial era, we'd have to take a gently feminine stroll through the rose garden at this point."

"Roses wouldn't be so bad," said Dewey, trotting meekly along behind her newfound friends. She noticed with a pang of regret that the quiet waiters were now bringing out brandy for the gentlemen—by the looks of it, hundred-year-old Napoleon. Shaking her head, she followed the other women up the stairs to a large room with flowered wallpaper and chintz-covered sofas. There she found Jane Duncan and Maria Porter, who had secured a small rank of sofas near one of the front windows.

"Well!" exclaimed Jane. "How did you enjoy that?"

"Yeah," put in Maria. "Wasn't it kind of neat and kind of *weird*, Mrs. James?"

"Odd. Decidedly odd," agreed Dewey. "I only wish that my friend George Farnham could have been here for that meal."

"He's the one that cooks so well, right?" asked Jane.

"Oh, yes, indeed. He's our leading gourmet in Hamilton. Our only gourmet, in fact." Dewey laughed gently.

"And he's in love with you, isn't he, Dewey?"

Dewey blushed. "Good heavens, Jane."

"Say no more. I can see that he is. Well, well. It's high time you began to live it up a little, my dear."

"I *am* living it up, Jane," replied Dewey with a smile.

"Are you, now? So glad to hear it."

They were soon joined by Andrea Follet and Sophia Fuller, who seemed to have taken rather a liking to Dewey.

"I wonder what they're up to at Lady Catherine de-Burgh's tonight?" asked Andrea Follet with a glint of mischief in her eye.

"So elegant, *so* condescending," put in Dewey with a laugh. "On the other hand, I just know that that newspaper reporter was going to light that dreadful stogie of his and ruin the Napoleon brandy. If only it were a decent cigar, I wouldn't mind so much." Dewey's late husband, Brendan James, had smoked the occasional cigar; but he had chosen well, and Dewey had never minded them.

"Stinky," agreed Sophia Fuller, pulling up a small footstool and sinking into it gratefully. She kicked off her shoes and wiggled her toes.

"Pity about the brandy, though," said Andrea Follet in a musing tone. "I mean, that they won't give *us* any."

"Oh, won't they, now?" retorted Jane Duncan. With a wink for Dewey, she signaled to a black-suited servant, who approached with dignified steps. "Would you mind, awfully, sir," she asked, her voice arch, "if we asked you to bring us a little refreshment?"

The man smiled benevolently upon Jane. "Certainly, madam."

"That's lovely. I think we'd like you to bring us a nice bottle of that brandy that the men are being served."

"Of the brandy, madam?" he asked, as though unfamiliar with brandy.

"Yes. The Napoleon. And five snifters."

"Yes, madam."

"See how easy that was?" asked Jane, pleased with herself.

"Perfect," agreed Andrea Follet. With a look at Sophia's feet, she kicked off her own shoes.

"And we don't mind if we never see another meal, not for a week, do we?" Jane went on.

"Two weeks," agreed Dewey.

"Three," said Maria Porter, who was semirecumbent on a chaise longue. "Maybe three and a half."

The shuffling butler soon reappeared, a dubious look upon his face and a dusty green bottle on his tray. As he poured the brandy, Dewey noted with interest a small storm brewing just across the room.

Lainie Guiles had just arrived from somewhere. She looked around for a place to perch, but most of the seats were taken; and she seemed on the point of leaving again when Marge Gantry entered.

For a moment the two women regarded each other coolly. Then Marge's emotions seemed to get the better of her. Dewey, intrigued, strained to listen over the chatter of the twenty or so women in the room. Jane Duncan, following Dewey's eye, watched the scene go forth with interest. The conversation between the two was inaudible; but the animosity on Marge Gantry's part came through loud and clear. Dewey and Jane looked on as Marge Gantry's face became once more suffused with red blotches. Lainie Guiles, for her part, looked unruffled; but then, she almost always looked unruffled. Dewey had remarked the almost lizardlike composure of the Bently director's features. It would be difficult to know if anything actually reached her, for she never lost the glassy-eyed stare that Dewey had noticed this morning.

Lainie Guiles, apparently unaware that every woman in the room was watching her, walked coolly to a small divan in the corner and sat down. She was quickly followed by another woman, who pulled up a chair and began to talk to her earnestly.

"Bad blood, I imagine," Jane remarked at last.

"Yes, indeed," replied Dewey. "I wonder what it's all about."

"I would guess that it's all about power—and the Bently Foundation. Wouldn't you?"

"Yes," agreed Dewey. "I daresay you're right. Too bad, though. It has been such a lovely party."

7

THE DAY FOLLOWING the Pinkie Dinner brought with it an eerie sense of déjà vu. Once more there was chaos and bad feeling at the Bently Foundation; and once more Lainie Guiles hadn't turned up for work.

Jane and Dewey had dropped in at about a quarter past ten to congratulate Lainie and her staff on the events of last night. The dinner had gone off superbly; the food had been remarkable, if not altogether interesting, and everyone had had a marvelous time. Donald Brewster had been interviewed by all the members of the press in attendance, and he had even been approached by the director of the New York Classical Drama Festival to discuss working on an updated version of *Medea* for the next season.

When Jane and Dewey arrived, they found everyone in high dudgeon. Terry Fenhaden, his muffinlike face showing the deepest possible discontent, was in the throes of a bitter argument with Lawrence Montrose.

"I'm not your bloody *errand* boy, Montrose," they heard Fenhaden say firmly. "And I'm not going to go chasing all over New York looking for Lainie Guiles. I did that yesterday."

"You'll do it, Fenhaden," replied Montrose.

"Forget it. Send Marge."

"Marge is out with the flu."

"She was perfectly well enough last night. Well, then, Maria can go."

"Maria is needed here."

"Good morning, Lawrence!" interposed Jane Duncan brightly.

"Hello, Jane." Montrose scowled at her, intensified his scowl for Dewey, and returned his attention to Fenhaden. "Just do as I ask you, Fenhaden."

Jane Duncan didn't much care for these scenes, a fact she had mentioned to Lawrence Montrose just last night. With a start he appeared to recollect Jane's sentiments and her million-dollar endowment, for he suddenly made a visible effort to pull himself together, rounding smoothly on the two ladies.

"Sorry. Hello, Jane," he repeated in a warmer voice, permitting himself a handsome smile.

"That's better, Lawrence. What is everyone up in arms about this morning?"

"Lainie Guiles," answered Terry Fenhaden bitterly, "is playing the princess again." He ignored the warning glare from Montrose. "And I'm damned if I'm going to dance to her little tune." He stomped off in the direction of his own office.

"Never mind Terry," said Montrose smoothly, taking Jane by the elbow. "I hope you enjoyed our little festivities last night, Mrs. James," he added with a bow.

Maria Porter raised an eyebrow at Dewey, who laughed. "I've certainly never seen so much food at one meal," Dewey replied. "And Maria was an invaluable guide, pointing out all the high-hats and luminaries for me."

"Ah, yes." Montrose was gratified. "We do certainly attract them at the Pinkie Dinner. It must have been very interesting for you—the cream of New York's artistic and intellectual crowd."

"Yes," replied Dewey noncommittally, "it was quite a group." She thought of Howard Horde, and his half-smoked cigar, and his talk of incinerators. If he was the cream, who on earth could be the skim?

"Tell me, Lawrence," said Jane, "what's all this fuss about Lainie? Where is she?"

"That's the question. There's no answer at her house, and she hasn't called in."

"Perhaps she's playing hooky, tending to personal errands," Dewey suggested. "She must have been up to her eyeballs getting everything ready for the dinner."

"Yes, she has been," agreed Jane. "And really, Lawrence, the poor thing deserves a day off."

Montrose shook his head. "Not today she doesn't. We have to settle all the accounts for the party last night."

"Oh, pooh. That can wait." Jane took off her mink and tossed it casually on a hall chair. Dewey followed suit with her sturdy tweed coat, wondering what all the fuss was about. Surely there couldn't be pressing business for Lainie Guiles here today. Maybe Jane Duncan was right—maybe Lawrence Montrose was teetering on the brink of something, where Lainie was concerned.

The telephone rang in the front office, and Maria left to answer it, while Montrose led the two ladies to a small, prettily decorated morning room across the hall. Montrose was thoroughly pleased with the way the dinner had gone and preened over the many successful encounters he had had with some of New York's leading lights. Lawrence Montrose struck Dewey as a somewhat obtuse man; but she had to give him credit. He had evidently made the most of his moderate intelligence and his good looks. He was lucky to be tall; height, Dewey knew, almost always conferred power. And then, of course, there was his personal fortune—all inherited (according to Jane) but nonetheless a great opener of doors. Still, if what Jane told her was true, Montrose had done very well for the Bently Foundation.

As she listened to his conversation with Jane, Dewey reflected that Montrose was perfect for his job. He was cultivated to just the right degree, but not so polished that he would make potential contributors feel gauche. He was amiable, when he chose to be, and smart enough to get by; but there was no risk that his intelligence could be overpowering. Quite the contrary, actually, thought Dewey; when you talked to Lawrence Montrose, you quite inevitably had the sensation of being the more intelligent member of the conversation. That fact could be a valuable public-relations tool.

Montrose was talking to Jane about a woman with whom he had chatted last night. "Oh, yes, indeed," he was saying, "I had quite a conversation with Millicent Boone. She's such an old dear."

"Ah," said Jane, brightening. "Did you, now? Dewey, Millicent Boone was the divine old lady in the sequins. She's Boone's Woolens, you know, and an eccentric billionairess. Ninety-two years old, I think. No children, no living family members at all."

"Aha," said Dewey, comprehending the appeal of Millicent Boone. She wished that there were such billionairesses in Hamilton to tap for funding for her little library.

"What did dear old Millicent have to say, Lawrence?" Jane asked. "Is she going to make a little present to us?"

"Well, she wanted to know all about the possibilities for a worthwhile placement of funds. I talked to her at length about a trusteeship—"

Maria Porter reappeared suddenly in the foyer, her face pale. "Mr. Montrose—"

Montrose ignored her. "Not that there's really room on the board, but you never know. Two of the terms will be up in January, and I, of course, wanted her to feel—"

"Mr. Montrose." Maria was firm.

"What *is* it, Maria?"

"It's Lydia—Lainie's cleaning lady. She's on the phone."

"Cleaning lady? Tell her to do the windows." He chuckled at his own little joke and turned once more to Jane.

"I wanted Millicent to feel, naturally, that she could offer more than just her millions."

"Mr. Montrose, I think you had better take this call." Maria Porter's face was drained of all its color, and her voice was uncommonly serious. Dewey, suddenly concerned, crossed to her and took her hand.

"What is it, child?"

"It's about Lainie," said Maria firmly. "Lydia is on the phone. I think Mr. Montrose should speak to her."

"Good Lord, girl, take a message." Montrose waved a hand and shook his head, every inch the important man-about-town. "Come sit down, Mrs. James."

Dewey ignored him. "Maria?"

"Lainie's dead, Mrs. James. I thought perhaps Mr. Montrose would want to know. You tell him for me, will you, when he can find a minute to listen?" She turned on her heel and walked sturdily away.

They were all clustered now in Lainie's office, this strange little group. Lawrence Montrose was pacing, telephone receiver in hand. "How sure are you? . . . All right, all right. Listen. Stay *right* there. Don't move—don't do anything." He covered the mouthpiece and looked up at Jane Duncan, who was perched tensely on the leather chesterfield against the wall. "I can hardly understand a word this woman says. Why don't they ever speak English?"

"Here, Lawrence, let me." Jane rose and took the telephone receiver from him, then spoke for five minutes in fluent Spanish. When she was through, she handed the phone back to Montrose. "Lydia seems to think that Lainie has committed suicide. I've told her to stay right there. You tell her again."

"Dear heaven," said Dewey. "How terribly tragic."

Montrose grabbed for the phone. "We ought to call a doctor."

"Who?" asked Jane.

"Well, *I* don't know who. Wait." He looked up at Maria. The color had gone from her face entirely. "Maria—who's Lainie's doctor?"

"I don't know," answered Maria mechanically. "I could look it up—"

"Never mind." Montrose was brusque. "Jane, just name me a doctor."

"Herbert Von Cassel," replied Jane Duncan, for once nearly at a loss for words.

"Von Cassel," Montrose repeated mechanically. Maria scrambled frantically for the telephone directory. She found Von Cassel's number quickly and handed him the book, and Montrose read the number off to the woman on the other end. "And stay there. Just—I don't *care*. For God's sake, stay there. Someone will be along shortly." He hung up.

There was a long silence. Finally Montrose spoke again. "I suppose we had better go there." He looked at Jane Duncan, who nodded.

"Yes, I think that's wise." She rose and pulled on her coat, and they headed for the door.

"I'm coming, too, Mrs. Duncan," Maria said firmly. She had regained her composure.

"No, you're not, young lady," Montrose answered firmly. "You stay put. We need you here." He looked at Dewey James. "Mrs. James, will you be good enough to keep Maria company, please?"

"Of course, Mr. Montrose," replied Dewey.

"Thank you. Now—Jane?"

"Yes, let's go, Lawrence."

They departed, leaving Maria and Dewey to wait.

Maria went to her small office and sat down at her desk. Dewey followed.

"Are you all right, my dear?"

"Yes, thank you," said Maria, controlling the quaver in her voice. "I'll be fine." She put her head in her hands and sat motionless at her desk. Dewey pulled up a small chair and sat quietly with her.

"Maria," said Dewey, breaking the silence at last," I know that this is none of my business. But I wonder—that is to say—in cases like this, oughtn't one to call the police?"

Maria lifted her head and regarded Dewey with surprise. The look changed swiftly to admiration. The old lady was really on the ball. She nodded.

"What's Lainie's address?" Dewey asked.

Maria spun quickly through her Rolodex and read out the address.

Dewey, nodding, jotted it down. Then she reached for Maria's telephone and dialed 911.

8

AN HOUR PASSED; and then half an hour more. Dewey and Maria spent the time comfortably enough, although Maria's distress was still palpable. Terry Fenhaden had disappeared; sometime during the hubbub, Dewey had heard him leaving. The sound hadn't registered at the time, but he evidently had taken off in a fit of pique. She wondered idly if they ought to try to find him; then she settled on the solution of leaving a note for him on his desk.

When she returned to Lainie's office, she sat with Maria a while longer in tense silence. At long last the telephone rang; it was Jane Duncan.

"Dewey," she said, sounding more breathless than usual, "there are policemen here. They said they had been called. Did *you* call them?"

"Naturally, Jane," replied Dewey evenly. "I telephoned. One does need to inform the authorities in such cases. And since—"

"Thank *heaven* for you, Dewey," Jane interrupted. "We might all have been arrested or something if it hadn't been for your quick thinking. Now—I need you to come here at once. Bring Maria Porter with you. There's a sergeant or something, maybe he's a lieutenant, who needs to have a talk with Maria. Will you do that?"

Dewey, with a thoughtful look at Maria, acquiesced.

They switched on the answering machine and put on their coats. As they departed, the huge front door of the Bently Mansion swung shut with a cultivated, soft thud. Maria locked it carefully and they made their way the three short blocks to Lainie Guiles's apartment.

The director of the Bently Foundation had lived and died in one of those anonymous white-brick apartment towers that intrude without apology into the charm and sophistication of New York's older residential districts. The building fronted Third Avenue, which at this time of day was thick with traffic and overhung with the exhaust of thousands of buses and taxis. A sallow, frightened-looking doorman greeted Maria and Dewey and directed them to apartment 7-D.

The apartment was fairly large, by New York standards, although Dewey—born and bred in the countryside and the open air—considered it amazing that people could make a home for themselves in such confining, boxlike surroundings. The living room was prettily furnished with expensive antiques; at the back were French doors that opened onto a tiny terrace. In an alcove, next to windows that looked out into a courtyard, were a mahogany dining table and a small sideboard. In another alcove on the opposite wall were several bookshelves, some small cherry filing cabinets, and a glass-topped desk stocked with stationery, a silver cup holding pens and pencils, a few reference books, and a small computer. Next to the computer was a beautiful blown-glass vase containing three yellow roses. A small hallway led to the bedroom and bathroom beyond.

For all of its antiques and pretty furnishings, the place struck Dewey as being peculiarly devoid of personality. It seemed to have been inhabited by a cipher.

Lawrence Montrose was pacing up and down the length of a Persian rug, under careful observation of a small, frightened-looking woman with bright red hair. This, thought Dewey, was undoubtedly Lydia. She was seated stiffly upright on a chintz-covered sofa in the living room.

One hand idly rested on a small needlepoint pillow. "IF YOU DON'T HAVE ANYTHING NICE TO SAY," read the legend on the pillow, "COME AND SIT NEXT TO ME."

Jane Duncan, still wrapped in mink, was squaring off with a young, beefy, uniformed policeman. He was nodding distractedly as she chattered away at him. Dewey overheard a fragment of their conversation and understood that Jane was interceding for Lydia, in the murky matter of her status as an undeclared wage-earner on American soil. No wonder the woman looked frightened; she was probably terrified of the immigration authorities. Jane would handle it, thought Dewey fondly. Jane always found a way to help in situations like this.

In the far corner, near the alcove that did service as a dining room, was a tall man who, in spite of his plain clothes, was evidently a member of New York's Finest. He looked up with curiosity at Maria and Dewey.

Everyone exchanged introductions of a sort, and the police sergeant, after a nod from the plainclothes officer, broke away from Jane Duncan to dismiss Montrose and the cleaning woman. Lydia thanked Jane profusely in Spanish, and then hurried away. Montrose, however, objected.

"As a trustee of the foundation, Sergeant, it is my duty to remain on hand while you question Maria."

"No, I don't think so," replied the beefy sergeant. "Do you think so, Lieutenant?" He appealed to the tall man, who had introduced himself to Dewey and Maria as Lieutenant Spangle. Spangle shook his head.

"See, there?" the sergeant went on. "We've got these nice ladies to look after your young friend, sir. We'll call you if we need you." He sent Montrose packing and shut the door firmly behind him.

Lieutenant Spangle took Maria gently by the elbow and guided her to the dining table. His manner with her was considerate but firm, and there was no mistaking his authority—despite the somewhat comical effect of a huge, drooping walrus mustache that embellished the lower half of his face. He was efficient and friendly as he worked to put Maria at her ease; and Maria—who had so far borne up very well—allowed her lower lip to tremble under the kindness of Lieutenant Spangle's gaze.

"Dewey, dear," said Jane Duncan, leading the way to a pair of brocaded armchairs in the living room, "this is just terrible. So sad, you know."

Dewey took a seat and nodded. "They are certain it's suicide?"

"Well," said Jane in a low voice, looking over toward the table where Maria and Spangle were talking, "yes, I think so. That is, there were pills and so forth. A bottle of some kind of wine. And there's a note, apparently—not exactly a note, but a message from Lainie." She nodded grimly in the direction of the desk and computer.

"A note on the computer?" asked Dewey, disbelieving.

"Lainie always struck me as being very modern and up-to-date," replied Jane sadly. "I didn't know that she would be so *very* modern, though."

"How strange," remarked Dewey. Then she motioned to Jane for silence and settled back into the armchair to listen to the conversation going forth in the dining alcove. The lieutenant was asking Maria for details of her last exchange with Lainie.

"Well, perhaps you don't know what her plans were last night, after the dinner," the lieutenant said kindly, "but maybe you can help us guess. Let's start with any telephone calls, Miss Porter. Especially calls of a personal nature. As Ms. Guiles's assistant, surely you were privy to much of her personal life."

"Well, sure," agreed Maria. "That is, Lainie sort of confided in me, a little bit." She smiled thinly. "Not the details."

"Can you tell us, please, what she did yesterday?"

Maria recounted the events of the morning—Lucas Hanover's visit, and Madeline Hoffman's. Lainie had left the Bently Foundation shortly after noon, spending the rest of the day at the J. Preston Palmer House, making certain that everything was ready for the big event.

"Nothing struck you as unusual?"

"No. I mean, everybody was kind of on edge because there was a lot to do; but I don't think Lainie was worried or anything."

"All right, then. How about the day before? Was there anything that happened to upset her? Tell me about her telephone calls, for instance. I assume you handle those."

"Yeah. Let's see—the ones I put through, anyway." Maria closed her eyes briefly, thinking. "She had three calls from Mr. Montrose, about the Pinkie Dinner. She talked to Mrs. Hoffman, the caterer, about the caviar, because we were trying to get a discount. Mrs. Duncan called"—Maria hesitated slightly, glancing over in Jane and Dewey's direction—"and Mr. Lippincott."

"Mr. Lippincott?"

"You know. Hayden Lippincott, the actor."

"They were friends?"

"Well—" Maria bit her lip. "She was kind of mad at him, I think. But that was nothing new."

"They were more than just friends, then." Spangle leaned heavily back in his chair and folded his arms, nodding quietly.

"Well, sure, everyone knew that. They dated for a really long time, like a year or something, but I think Lainie was kind of fed up with him." She seemed to hesitate.

Spangle urged her on. "They talked on Wednesday?"

"They talked every day," replied Maria.

"And they were on good terms?"

"Well, they were having a little bit of an argument. On Wednesday, anyway, they were having an argument. I don't know for sure about yesterday. She wasn't really mad—just annoyed, really."

"Do you know why?"

"Uh, no."

"But you have an idea?"

"Well—he was kind of possessive, I think. She told me he was always snooping on her, wanting to know where she went and what she did."

"And she considered this curiosity abnormal?"

"Well, only after they had broken up about a hundred times. I think it got to be too much for her, you know?"

"I think I know, Miss Porter," said the lieutenant with a smile for his sergeant, who was seated at the end of the table, taking notes. "Now—at the office, yesterday. Was there anything unusual going on? Something that might have upset Ms. Guiles?"

"No. It was pretty chaotic, and Lainie was late getting to work, and everybody was pretty mad at her, but that's just because we still had a lot to do for the dinner."

"What about the day before? Anything unusual happen? Did she seem depressed or out of sorts?"

"No. I left about five-thirty, maybe a little after, and she was still there, but I think she was getting ready to leave."

"What was she working on?"

Maria looked thoughtful. "She had just finished figuring out where everybody was going to sit at the Pinkie Dinner when Hayden Lippincott called. She talked to him, and then she asked me about what time Mr. Hanover was coming in. He's an art dealer. He was at the Pinkie Dinner last night, and I think she talked to him there."

"This Hanover had an appointment for some reason?"

"Yeah. I mean, I think he was getting set to buy something from the Bently Collection. That's what Lainie had to talk to Marge about, I think. She had to tell her about it."

Dewey suddenly comprehended—or thought she comprehended—the strange contretemps between the two colleagues last night. Marge Gantry, curator of the Bently Collection, hadn't been pleased, somehow, about the sale of a painting to Lucas Hanover. Odd.

"I see." Spangle leaned back easily in his chair, stroking

at the huge tawny creature on his face. "Last night at the dinner, did it strike you that she was in any way upset?"

"No."

"And you had no hint that there was anything truly wrong?"

"Uh, no. Nothing big. Just little annoyances."

"I see." Spangle rose. "I think that will do. Thank you for coming here, Miss Porter." He nodded to the sergeant, who put away his notebook and stood to escort Maria to the door.

Dewey and Jane rose to follow. As Jane buttonholed the beefy sergeant for one last round of agonized questions, Dewey gave in to an impulse. She looked over her shoulder. Spangle was near the front door, having a last word with Maria. Dewey took three short steps across the room to the desk alcove and, bending at the waist, squinted at the screen of the computer.

Some words—gray-white on a dark gray background— glowed up at her. She read them with interest.

This may come as a surprise to people, but it's no surprise to me that I should take this way out of things. Maybe I just wasn't up to it all. Thank you all and goodbye.

"Mrs. James?" Spangle called from across the room. The sergeant, following his superior's gaze, strode manfully. Dewey straightened and put on an innocent face.

"Oh!" she said. "Terribly sorry. I didn't mean to be nosy."

"You'll have to leave now, ma'am," said the sergeant forcefully, taking her by the elbow.

"Oh, yes, indeed. I was just coming." She adjusted her coat and shook off the sergeant's grasp. "Coming, Jane," she said to her friend and hurried across the room.

9

OVER DINNER AT Jane's house that evening, the two old friends filled Donald Brewster in on the events of the day. Dewey had noted, when Brewster came to call later that afternoon, that the playwright appeared disproportionately shocked by the news of Lainie's death. By dinnertime, however, he seemed to have regained his spirits.

"I knew her fairly well, you know, Dewey," Brewster remarked as they were finishing their dessert. He glanced at Jane Duncan, radiant in the candlelight. "Because of Hayden Lippincott, of course—that is, because she and he were a pair for so long. He has been in my last two plays, you know. Lainie used to come and watch our rehearsals for *Don Juan* sometimes. Knew a thing or two about the theater and knew how to deal with Lippincott. Who is a handful."

"Yes, I can imagine he is," agreed Dewey, who was predisposed to take most actors with a grain of salt. "Quite handsome and successful—in my experience, that can be a lethal combination."

Jane giggled. "In mine, too—with one exception." She reached out and took Brewster's hand. "You haven't let your good looks and your success spoil you, have you, my darling?"

Brewster winked at Dewey. "I keep the rotten core of me well hidden," he remarked lightly, giving Jane's hand a

74

squeeze. "But wait until we're married, my dear, and you shall know all."

Dewey smiled benevolently on the lovebirds, her mind elsewhere. Jane noticed her distraction.

"Whatever is on your mind, Dewey? Don't tell me you suspect Donald is really after my money."

"What?" asked Dewey. "Oh—sorry. Don't be silly, Jane. You'll set Donald's heart against me, and I couldn't bear that."

"Well, then. Suppose you tell me what *is* on your mind. You've been a positive sleepwalker all day, ever since we got back from that tragic business at Lainie's."

"Jane is right, you know, Dewey," added Donald, looking at her intently. "You do seem to have something on your mind. Is everything all right? I hope all this rushing around New York isn't too much for you."

"Oh, no." Dewey laughed. "It's a vacation, Donald, and couldn't be more relaxing. But—"

"But *what*, Dewey?" Jane insisted impatiently. "I know! Dewey, you're holding out on us. You are convinced that Lainie Guiles didn't kill herself, aren't you? Donald, I have told you that Dewey is rather a celebrity in her hometown because she has solved *three* murders that had the police stumped. Totally stumped."

"Well, now—" Dewey began to protest.

"Yes, indeed," said Brewster, rising to fetch the brandy bottle from the sideboard. "In fact, Dewey, I heard your name in connection with that lovely dancer, Jenny Riley, more than a year ago. Before I even really knew Jane."

"Oh!" Dewey was surprised momentarily, until she recollected that Jenny Riley had been famous in New York as well as in her hometown of Hamilton. Jenny Riley's death had stumped the Hamilton Police, and Dewey had been happy to help them out of their difficulties and solve the murder.

"Yes, Dewey, it's true," said Jane warmly. "Just in case

you think you're *not* a New York celebrity—well, you are. Just like Donald.''

''Heavens,'' muttered Dewey.

''Out with it, Dewey,'' commanded Jane.

Donald handed out the snifters of brandy, eyeing Dewey closely. ''Yes, Dewey,'' he echoed in a hearty voice, ''by all means, out with it. Let's hear what you have to say about all of this.'' He resumed his seat and cocked an eyebrow at her.

''Good gracious!'' exclaimed Dewey. ''Well—it's just that I thought that business of the farewell note was mighty strange. Have you ever heard of anything so absurd?''

''What was absurd about leaving a note?''

''On a computer screen?'' Dewey asked, indignant. ''That young woman had plenty of beautiful monogrammed stationery, right there on her desk. I saw it. So—it struck me as odd, that's all.''

''Maybe she types better than she writes. Some people do, you know,'' said Jane, ''because they get kind of addicted to typing. Donald, for instance. His handwriting has gone to hell in a handbasket since he got himself a computer.''

''Er—yes, kind of you to point that out, my dear,'' replied Brewster.

''Well, it *has*, Donald. Not your writing, but your penmanship. Because you never use a pen any longer.'' She turned to Dewey. ''So. You think there is some funny business, don't you, Dewey?''

''Indeed I do,'' she nodded.

''We must tell that detective,'' proposed Jane. ''What was his name? Dingle?''

''Spangle,'' amended Dewey.

''Spangle, that's right. You're *so* clever, Dewey. We'll call him at home, right away,'' responded Jane. She stood up, then sat down again in a hurry. ''We'll never be able to track him down. He probably lives in Brooklyn or Staten

Island or somewhere like that, where there are probably a thousand Spangles. I only have the Manhattan directory.''

Dewey suppressed a giggle.

"Relax, my dear," interposed Brewster, taking Jane's hand once more. He turned to Dewey. "With all due respect, Dewey—"

"Oh, yes, Donald. I couldn't agree more. This is New York, after all, and not Hamilton." She smiled. "I doubt that Lieutenant Spangle would welcome any suggestions from me. He's no Fielding Booker, I'm certain." She smiled and sipped at her brandy.

Lieutenant Francis Spangle was an unusually well-informed man, with a mind both deeply curious and strongly inclined to remember details. This fact, resented by many of his fellow officers, had helped him to advance fairly swiftly in the force—until those people just ahead of him on the ladder of authority had begun to feel insecure. When this happened, of course, Spangle's rise in the ranks had halted abruptly, and there had even been talk of assigning him to the Family Disturbances Unit or transferring him to desk duty. Thus are we all at the mercy of our talents.

At his office on the morning following Lainie Guiles's death, Spangle had turned to a report compiled by Sergeant Skinner. It was a rundown on all the people who had been in daily contact with Lainie Guiles, and all the people who had been at the Bently Foundation during the morning. Spangle had no reason to think there had been foul play; in fact, his own report concluded that Lainie Guiles had died by her own hand. Spangle, however, liked to be thorough, and he liked to know whom he was dealing with. In case any little problem should arise down the road.

In the report there was a profile on Dewey James, obtained by fax from the Hamilton authorities. Accompanying the profile was a note, in a florid, old-fashioned hand, from Captain Fielding Booker of the Hamilton police. It read, in part, "Despite my personal feelings of friendship and esteem for Mrs. James, I feel it my duty to forewarn you that she likes to take an interest in police affairs which are, frankly speaking, none of her business. If she is in some way connected with the problem you have on your hands, I suggest you be very firm with her, or you will find yourselves the recipients of all manner of unwanted advice."

"Oh, brother," Spangle muttered as he tossed the report on his desk. He picked up his telephone and spoke to the desk sergeant on duty. "You say there's a Mrs. James here to see me?" he asked.

"Yes, sir." The sergeant on duty at the precinct house looked up at the prim figure of Dewey James, seated quietly on a bench, apparently unperturbed by the chaos of her surroundings. "She says it's important, sir, and that she can wait all day if necessary."

"No need for that. Send her in, Sergeant."

"Yes, sir."

Dewey was shown into Spangle's office—a small, glassed-in cubicle at the back of a large, busy room. She took a seat and smiled modestly up at the lieutenant.

"Thank you very much for seeing me, Lieutenant," she said.

"No problem."

"I know that as a visitor to your city, I really have no claim on your time—"

"On the contrary. New York has a duty and an obligation to its visitors, to see that they enjoy themselves when they come here. It's important to us. But suppose you tell me what it is I can do for you."

"It's about that young woman," Dewey began.

"That much I figured."

"Forgive my sticking my nose in. But, Lieutenant, you talked to Maria. Lainie Guiles had nothing on her mind, no troubles, no worries—except to see that all went smoothly for the big awards dinner last night."

"We don't know that for certain. And I'd say, you know,

that maybe her death proves otherwise. Suicide usually means somebody's got something on their mind.''

"Well, yes—naturally I would agree. But you see, Lieutenant, you have brought me to the crux of the matter at hand. I am rather convinced, you know, that Lainie Guiles did not kill herself.''

"No?'' Spangle raised an eyebrow and put his hands behind his head. The cop in this old bat's hometown had been right, all right. Unwanted advice. Spangle had nothing more urgent on for this morning, however, so he was prepared to ride it out. "You have some reason for thinking this, I guess, although you never even met the lady.''

"Yes—well, perhaps it sounds preposterous, but I merely wanted to point out, in case you haven't considered it, that the suicide note was extremely odd.''

"Was it, now?''

"Well—yes. In the first place, what person, man or woman, would just leave an important note like that sitting on a computer screen?''

"Seems as good a place as any,'' remarked Spangle.

"No, I disagree,'' said Dewey firmly. "You see, there was a printer right there, next to the computer. So if for some reason she felt she ought to type her farewell message, I think it's most odd that she didn't bother to make a printed copy.''

"Hmmm.''

"Besides—now, I didn't get a very good look at the machine, and of course I have no idea what kind it is or anything like that. But Lieutenant Spangle, I am a librarian. And at my little library we have—er—recently gone electronic. Do I make myself clear?''

Spangle stifled a yawn. "You got a computer in your library.''

"Yes, that's exactly right. And I know that when a person types something up on that screen, it isn't permanent, not permanent at all—not unless he pushes some buttons that will keep it from vanishing altogether, if the electricity should go off or something. Or so I have been told.''

"Yes, I know how they work." Spangle gestured to the machine on a table behind him. "We even got one here, believe it or not, but it's broken. Of course." He grinned.

"Well, my point is, Lieutenant, that a young woman saying goodbye to the world would hardly take that risk. That her suicide note would vanish."

Spangle stroked his vast mustache and leaned forward. "Look at it another way, Mrs. James. That lady was out of it. The autopsy report here''—he poked a file folder with his finger—''shows that she had consumed an enormous quantity of pills, in conjunction with nine ounces of red wine. A good Burgundy, but a fatal mixture.''

"Well, yes. Naturally it would be fatal, wouldn't it, if someone had wished her dead?"

"No, no, no. If she forgot to print the thing out, or to make a permanent file, that doesn't necessarily mean anything. Nothing. Because she was out of it, really out of it.''

"I only *suggest*, Lieutenant, that if she had been so far gone as to be unable to write, or to forget to print the document, she would hardly have had the mental wherewithal to turn on the computer and create the document in the first place. If you follow me."

"Hmm," said Spangle. He leaned back, considering the point.

"What is more," Dewey went on, pursuing this opening with energy, "I did steal a little peek at that note of hers."

"Yes, ma'am. We noticed you noticing, so to speak."

"Yes," replied Dewey firmly. "And I consider the thing to be highly suspect."

"The note?"

"Yes. It had nothing in it, nothing at all, to suggest a personality at work."

"Well, Mrs. James, by all accounts Lainie Guiles wasn't much of a writer. Now, I've seen some suicide notes where the people go on and on for pages, never letting up with the guilt-tripping. But I've seen some short ones, too. This one didn't strike me as being off, in any way.'' He touched the tip of his nose. ''I sniff this stuff out for a living, Mrs. James.''

''Yes, and I can tell that you are *very* good at your job, too. But, Lieutenant, it was all so vague and hurried-sounding. I don't know—I merely offer these suggestions in case you had planned to consider the matter closed. That is to say, perhaps you ought to ask your pathologists to look very carefully for some sign of a struggle.'' Dewey rose and pulled her coat around her. ''I'm off, now,'' she said with a smile, ''and won't be back to bother you, because I am very sure that you are the kind of young man who likes to cover all the angles. You won't need any prodding from me, I'm certain. You'll just naturally check to make sure that her fingerprints hadn't been wiped off the keyboard, or anything like that.'' Dewey smiled and departed.

Spangle, tugging on the droopy ends of his mustache, watched her go.

''Damn,'' he breathed at last.

If it had just been his own instinct prodding him, he would have filed it. Cases like this could be impossible to prove, and there had been nothing unusual at the scene. Nothing to indicate that another person had been present. Spangle had looked it all over carefully, and the doctor, Von Cassel, had agreed with him. But it was true, there was something tugging at the back of his mind. He pulled toward him the file folder marked ''L.S. Guiles/S. 173 NYPD.'' The batty old lady had read his mind. He rang for Sergeant Skinner.

The lieutenant tapped the folder and looked at his sergeant.

''You think this lady killed herself?''

''Sure. You know women.'' The sergeant leaned back in a creaky wooden chair and rolled up his shirtsleeves.

"Most of the women I know don't go around killing themselves."

"Yeah—well, this one's rich, or in with a rich crowd. She gets dumped by her famous actor boyfriend, and from what I can make out she wasn't doing too hot at her job. So she offs herself, and bingo!—no more problems."

Spangle shook his head. "I don't agree."

"But, Lieutenant, yesterday—"

"That was yesterday, Skinner. This is today. Get to work. See what you can dig up. And get the morgue on the phone, pronto. Don't let 'em release the body until they check for signs that she may have put up some kind of struggle."

"You think somebody killed her?"

"I do."

"Jee-zus. All right. Just wait till Liz Smith gets hold of this one. You might get on their party list, Lieutenant."

10

"I'M SURE I had nothing whatsoever to do with it, Jane," said Dewey in a firm voice. The two friends were at Bergdorf's; Jane Duncan was shopping, and Dewey was taking it all in. Jane was evidently a familiar figure in the famous store; the salespeople greeted her with large smiles on every floor.

"Oh, go on, Dewey. Admit it. You went to see that Dingle—"

"Spangle. Lieutenant Spangle," Dewey corrected.

"Dingle, Spangle, bright shiny beads," sang Jane with a dismissive wave. "You went to see him, and *bingo!* He's changed his tune. You're a genius, Dewey."

"Good afternoon, Mrs. Duncan," said a small, dark saleswoman, approaching. "What can I do for you today?"

"Oh, hello, Myra. Meet my dearest friend, Dewey James. Dewey, Myra Spence looks after all my needs."

Dewey and the saleswoman exchanged polite greetings, and Jane Duncan went on. "We're looking for a *jolie* little frock," she said, putting one arm around Dewey's shoulders, "for Dewey."

"No, Jane," Dewey protested. "I have my good silk dress with me. We most certainly—"

"I insist, Dewey," replied Jane firmly. Myra Spence was busy sizing up the newcomer. "Something with pizzazz, not too dressy, for an afternoon wedding.'' Jane winked at Dewey, who did not protest further. She thought it best not to create a scene in front of the saleswoman. Besides, if Jane could afford to give a million dollars to the Bently Foundation, Dewey supposed that a dress would be no hardship. Besides—being a bridesmaid five times for the same person merited some sort of prize.

''I think I know just the thing,'' said Myra and toddled away.

''No need to mention *whose* wedding,'' whispered Jane with a laugh.

''No,'' agreed Dewey, chuckling. ''You'd never have a minute's peace from the press, Jane.''

''Too right.'' Jane led Dewey to a small, comfortably furnished lounge area, where they sat on an enormous, cushioned tuffet to await Myra Spence's reappearance. Jane returned to the topic of Lainie Guiles's death. ''Honest to God, Dewey. Lawrence Montrose has called an emergency meeting of the Bently Trustees for this afternoon. We have to figure out what to *do*, I suppose. From what I can gather, Lawrence has more or less stonewalled any police investigation, and we are all expected to do the same.''

''I can't imagine you'll get very far taking that approach,'' murmured Dewey. Her mind wasn't on murder; she was too busy taking in the glamorous women making their way through the store. It had been a long time since Dewey had shopped at Bergdorf's, and the spectacle was certainly a delight. It was just too bad, she thought, that they should all be in such a temper. Every single one of them had a scowl on her face. Dewey watched, amused and intrigued.

Jane sighed heavily. ''In any event, the official awarding of the Pinkie is to be postponed.''

''Well—that may help you out of your quandary, at least,'' Dewey remarked.

''I don't see how,'' complained Jane. ''It will just be worse, *after* we're married.''

"Not if everyone knows the decision was made before-hand. People have awfully short memories, Jane."

"I suppose you're right. Donald, at least, seems to be thrilled. Bless his heart—all he talks about is our wedding. As though we were youngsters."

"Indeed." Dewey wondered, not for the first time, what Donald Brewster's rush was. Perhaps he wanted to be sure to pin Jane down before her eye was caught by some other enthusiasm. Or perhaps he was just old-fashioned enough to consider marriage *de rigueur*. Dewey found it hard to believe, here among New York's arty and fast-moving crowd. But anything was possible. And he did *seem* like a very personable man—although there was naturally a chance that he was merely after Jane's money. A distinct possibility. Dewey didn't like to think about that. For all of Jane's many marriages, she was a very sensitive and devoted woman, and Dewey could tell that she was deeply in love with Donald Brewster.

Myra Spence returned with an armful of dresses for Dewey to try. The three women retreated to an outsize fitting room, where Dewey happily obliged her friend by being delighted with the most ordinary, and least expensive, of the bunch. It was a two-piece outfit of raspberry-colored silk, trimmed with black and purple braid at the collar. At least she would be able to wear it for special occasions in Hamilton, thought Dewey, with a regretful look at the price tag.

"Jane," said Dewey in a whisper when Myra Spence had departed, "are you *sure* about this?" She held up the discreet tag. The tiny figures after the dollar sign seemed to go on forever.

"Now, Dewey. As my bridesmaid, you have got to do whatever I say. It's my wedding, after all. And a person doesn't get married every day."

"No," agreed Dewey with a laugh. "Only every other day."

They bought the dress, arranged to have it delivered, and

stepped outside into the bright December sunshine. Jane proposed a walk uptown through Central Park, and Dewey, in need of some fresh air and sunshine, readily agreed. Jane led Dewey through the refurbished Children's Zoo, where most of the animals had retreated to warm winter quarters. A few hardy types—a polar bear, a gang of arctic seals, and a handful of penguins—provided a pleasant diversion for the two ladies as they ambled slowly past, then followed quiet paths through the nearly bare trees.

The two friends talked of this and that—of Brendan James, Dewey's late husband, and of the James's many adventures in the early years of their marriage. Jane Duncan, however, seemed unable to keep off the subject of Lainie Guiles for long. "You suspect it was murder, don't you, Dewey?" she asked at last.

"Yes, I do," agreed Dewey reluctantly. "Tell me, Jane," she went on. "What was she like?"

"Odd," replied Jane Duncan firmly. "For the first few months that I sat on the board, you know, I thought she was merely shy. But before long I began to feel differently. She had some sort of agenda, I think. Her manner—the way she presented herself to the world—seemed very much at odds with the heart of her. She was like a brittle shell, almost, a fancy shell, with a plain old hermit crab inside."

"Ah," remarked Dewey. "I had somewhat the same feeling at her apartment. As though she inhabited it but didn't live there. Everything was pretty enough, but in an odd way it all seemed to be for show. No 'there' there, as they say."

"I agree," said Jane warmly. "And I think that a woman so meticulously on display wouldn't be moved to kill herself."

"Well, how does one ever know what prompts people to suicide? The most unexpected people *do* kill themselves."

"Not that one, though. She was far too ambitious."

"Was she, now? Jane—was she the type of woman to make enemies?"

Jane laughed. "Enemies right and left, from what I've heard. Well, perhaps *enemy* is too strong a word; but there were plenty of old friends who were stranded by the wayside every time Lainie Guiles took a step up. She had an eye for the main chance, that woman, and was inclined to burn her bridges. Plus—if what Donald has told me is true—she really led Hayden Lippincott on. Used him terribly, then dropped him when he hit a patch of rough sailing."

"Ah. I know the type well," replied Dewey.

Jane Duncan looked at her watch and sped up her steps. "That meeting is going to start any minute, Dewey, and I have to be there. But listen—you simply *must* solve this case for us. If you can do it in Hamilton, where everyone knows you, then it will be a snap in New York. You can ask as many questions as you like, and nobody will have a clue that you're the sleuth on the trail. They'll just think you're a nosy lady from the boondocks."

"Yes, I suppose they will—for that's what I am, you know."

"Are you?" Jane's eyes twinkled. "Then it's a *perfect* setup." Jane beamed brightly at her friend, who laughed.

"The police have the matter well in hand, Jane," Dewey said finally. "Haven't you faith in your own police detectives?"

"No. None at all. That man Dingle is in way over his head, Dewey."

"Spangle," said Dewey.

"Dingle, Spangle. I promise to learn his name if you'll promise to solve his case for him." Jane tugged on Dewey's arm. "Agreed?"

"Jane, honestly. I—"

"You're just choosing to ignore the obvious, Dewey. Lieutenant Spangle, for all of his brains, hasn't got an entrée to the Bently crowd, Dewey. You must see that that's obvious. Whereas you *do* have."

"Jane, don't be preposterous. You make it all sound

so—so nineteenth century, like being invited to a party. Who fits in and who doesn't.''

''But that's just the point, Dewey. The Bently is nothing if not backward, persnickety, and completely out-of-date. There are plenty of people who can get a table at Lutèce at a moment's notice, who won't get the time of day at the Bently. That's just the way it is.''

Dewey shook her head. ''It all sounds fearfully snobbish to me, Jane. I'm almost surprised at you.''

''Well, you mustn't be. You see, the Bently is really a state of mind. Everything has its limitations and its drawbacks, Dewey, and there are plenty of exclusive clubs and charities. Especially the charities, in New York. At least the Bently is up front about its peculiarities.''

''Hmm.'' Dewey thought she saw what Jane meant. It was true that the Bently Foundation *was* an exceedingly peculiar organization; with its stuffy, silly rituals, and its caviar, and its general air of exclusivity. Yet there was probably room in the great city of New York, Dewey reflected, for an organization with an eccentric mind of its own. Certainly the Bently supported deserving artists, although none could be exactly described as starving. And it would be impossible to modernize the group. The only alternative to having the Bently function according to the rules laid down by Pincus Schermer Bently, IV, would be to end the Bently altogether.

Dewey reflected that the Bently had something in common with her hometown—which could also fairly be described as a state of mind. Hamilton had its fair share of interlopers, who wanted to ''improve'' the way Hamiltonians did things. Such intrusions were almost never successful. Never mind that Hamilton was an old-fashioned place; it suited Hamiltonians. The same could be said, Dewey supposed, for the Bently.

''Anyway,'' said Jane, breaking into Dewey's train of thought, ''there must be some way that you can get quickly to the bottom of all of this.'' They walked up an asphalt path that led out of Central Park onto Fifth Avenue; Dewey could see the Bently Mansion, two blocks up. "I'll tell you what," said Jane energetically. "You can come with me while I attend this *ghastly* meeting, and talk to the staff. Maria, of course, and that dreary Fenhaden, and poor Marge Gantry."

Dewey was shaking her head. "Come now, Jane. I can hardly go poking around where I've no business poking."

"But, Dewey!" protested Jane with the candor permitted only to the dearest of friends. "Why ever not? You do it all the time!"

11

THE BENTLY TRUSTEES—a select group who understood the Bently state of mind—were assembling about the large table in the mansion's dining room just as Dewey and Jane arrived.

"My money's on Terry Fenhaden," Jane whispered to Dewey, nodding in the direction of that young man's office. Then Jane slipped through the enormous sliding oak doors to the dining room and left Dewey to snoop about as she pleased.

Maria Porter was delighted to see Dewey and greeted her enthusiastically. "Hiya, Mrs. James," she called, waving the visiting librarian into her small but cheery office. "Still in town, huh?"

"Yes, indeed, Maria. I'm staying through the weekend." Dewey stepped in and looked about her. Maria had decorated her tiny quarters with posters from a variety of college theater productions. Dewey noted with particular interest the poster advertising a night of three one-act plays by seniors. Maria Porter was one of the contributing playwrights.

"You're a writer, aren't you?"

"Trying to be." Maria smiled mischievously. "I figure New York is as good a place as any to be an unacknowledged genius."

90

"Very true," replied Dewey, nodding. "You must meet a lot of very interesting and important people on the job. A chance to rub elbows with greatness."

"Yeah, right—or at least to make lunch reservations for greatness," said Maria with another grin. "How do you like New York? Is this your first visit?"

"Oh, heavens, no. My first visit in a good many years, however. It's a wonderful city, and certainly busier than I'm accustomed to."

"Yeah," agreed Maria, "it is busy. Busy with dead bodies all over the place, it seems like to me." She tossed back her thick, dark hair, and her black eyes shone. "Maybe I shouldn't say something like that."

"Well, my dear, you do sound a bit hard-hearted," replied Dewey. "On the other hand, I've never been one for sentiment where no true sentiment is felt. If you follow me."

"I agree," replied Maria, who looked chastened none-theless. "Maybe you'd like some coffee or tea or some-thing, Mrs. James."

"Why, yes. Thank you. I think a cup of tea might be just the thing. Jane took me to Bergdorf's, and I must recuper-ate."

"Oh, boy. I know what you mean. Cup of tea, coming right up." Maria stepped smartly off toward the kitchen, and Dewey took the opportunity to peek around the corner into Lainie Guiles's office. The desktop had been cleared off, and on one corner rested a cardboard box, over whose flaps projected pens and pencils and the top of an electric pencil sharpener. Somebody was moving fast, she reflected.

"Can I help you?" asked a voice behind Dewey. She turned. It was Terry Fenhaden, bearing another cardboard box in his arms.

"Oh, good gracious," said Dewey, in her best meek-old-lady voice. "So terribly sorry to be in your way, Mr., ah, Fenhaden, isn't it?"

"Right," said Terry Fenhaden, squeezing past Dewey

and depositing the box on Lainie's desk. He turned and looked at her with an interested, somewhat pitying stare. "You're Mrs. Duncan's friend, from out of town."

"Yes, that's right. How clever of you to remember. My name is Dewey James."

Dewey watched, transfixed, as Fenhaden began to unload the boxes. This young man surely worked quickly to fill the enticing void left by Lainie's death. Dewey was rather surprised that Lieutenant Spangle had given approval for Fenhaden to move in so soon. There was probably evidence of some sort in Lainie's office.

"Allow me to say, Mr. Fenhaden, how sorry I am about your loss."

"My loss?" The muffin-faced Fenhaden gave Dewey an uncomprehending cross-eyed stare, then returned to his unpacking.

"Well, the foundation's loss, at any rate," replied Dewey. "I gather Lainie had devoted many years of her life to the Bently."

"So she had," replied Fenhaden evenly.

"Yes. That kind of thing always seems so tragic to me. Imagine—spending a decade to help build up an exciting and deserving outfit such as the Bently, only to have a broken heart at the end of it all."

Fenhaden snorted. "Lainie? Lainie Guiles didn't have a heart, Mrs. James, so there was nothing to break."

"Oh. Dear me," said Dewey softly, sinking into the depths of a small leather sofa, the better to digest this further tragic information. Now, if Fenhaden wished her to go, he would be obliged to ask her to leave. Dewey settled in comfortably and folded her hands. "No heart, you say. Well, I wonder what can have driven her to take her own life in that way?"

Fenhaden, behind the desk, sat down with a proprietary air in the well-polished wooden Windsor chair that had been Pincus Schermer Bently's very own desk chair. Tradition (and the terms of Bently's will) dictated that this chair was for the exclusive use of the director of the foundation. Terry Fenhaden had had his eyes on the chair for a decade. He eased himself back into it, made a slight adjustment to the loose-fitting trousers of his custom-tailored Italian suit, and breathed out, a satisfied sigh.

"Oh, who knows?" Fenhaden replied at last. "Something got to her." He made a tent of his fingers and rested his chin on them, reflecting. "Although it's hard to imagine, really, anyone getting to her. She was a viperous little shrew." He smiled thinly and looked up at Dewey. "Do I shock you?"

"Oh, dear heavens, no," said Dewey, conscious that her admission must disappoint Fenhaden. "Believe me, I've known a few in my time such as you describe."

"Yeah. I guess they're all over."

"Yes, indeed. But I had understood from Mrs. Duncan that you and Lainie were friends, you see. My mistake."

"No—that was my mistake," corrected Fenhaden with a smile of grim amusement. "The friendship. A big mistake. With Lainie, the most surprising people qualified as friends. She put on a good act—kind of sucked you in. But she had no sense of loyalty, didn't seem to get what friendship was about. And by the time you realized what she was like, she was one up on you."

"Dear me," said Dewey sympathetically, with a shake of her head. She had certainly not expected such an outpouring of vitriol from this rather smug and unappealing young man; yet she knew that death by violence often toppled ordinary barriers of reticence.

What was more, it was easy to tell that Fenhaden didn't think Dewey a person of much consequence on his personal landscape. She was, for the moment, nothing more than a convenient receptacle for his bitter reflections. She was useful to him, filling the role of confessor in the way that a barber, or taxi driver, often does. A functional stranger. But strangers could be dangerous, Dewey reflected. It was best to know with whom you were dealing.

"Anyway," Fenhaden went on, "I suppose we should all be sorry that she killed herself. It could be an object lesson in self-satisfaction, I suppose. On the other hand, I'd lay you odds of a hundred to one that you won't find anyone who's sorry she's gone. And I'll be a far better director for the Bently. So I suppose the issue is closed."

For once, Dewey's dislike got the better of her garrulity. She was at a loss for words and had suddenly had quite enough of Terry Fenhaden's purring confidentiality. Out of the corner of her eye she saw Maria, tray in hand, making her way down the hall.

"Well, Mr. Fenhaden," said Dewey, rising, "I wish you success in your new position."

"Yeah," said Fenhaden, stroking the well-worn arms of the coveted Windsor chair. "Thanks." He nodded quietly to himself, seeming almost to forget Dewey, who slipped along to Maria's little office for tea.

"Mrs. James, that police detective was here all morning, asking questions and looking around. I think he thinks somebody *killed* Lainie." Maria poured out the tea. "Do you think so?"

Dewey accepted a cup and saucer from Maria. Crown Derby china, even for a casual visitor. The Bently Foundation was really quite a place. Dewey took a grateful sip of steaming tea. "It's certainly a possibility, Maria. But surely you know more about all this than I do."

"Hah. Not me—I'm pretty low on the totem pole around here, Mrs. James." She looked quickly out into the hallway, then closed her office door gently. "And I have a sneaking suspicion that I might even fall off that totem pole altogether," she said in a near whisper.

"But isn't everyone talking about it?"

"Nah. Marge just sulks upstairs in the gallery, and Terry hates me because Mr. Hanover, who's kind of a fancy art dealer, told me to call him Lucas—his first name, *you* know—but Terry has to call him Mr. Hanover. And Mr. Montrose hardly knows I'm alive. The only person who ever talked to me around here was Lainie. Even if she wasn't the nicest person in the whole world, she was okay to me." Maria smiled ironically. "I guess I just wasn't much of a threat to her."

"Dear heavens," muttered Dewey. This place was positively overrun with miserable politicking. It gave her the shivers.

"I know it doesn't sound very nice to say all of these things, Mrs. James, but I don't know why people always cover up for other people who are being stinky."

"That, Maria, is one of the great questions of all time. Playing the game—how far is too far? I am sure psychologists have been studying the phenomenon for years. At any rate, it certainly sounds as though this place has been in an uproar."

Maria looked thoughtful. "Especially lately. Maybe it's always like this right before the big Pinkie Dinner—I don't know. But everything was kind of in a panic."

"What sort of a panic?"

"Well, there was this big meeting yesterday morning. There were problems about money, I think. And Lainie and Mr. Montrose had a meeting to talk about expenses, and then Lainie had to tell everyone to be careful about how much money they spent. That made her unhappy—she really hated doing that kind of thing. Not because she felt bad, but because it made her kind of a target."

"Hmm." Dewey placed the teacup carefully on Maria's desk. "You mean the foundation was short of cash?"

"I guess so. Anyway, Terry seemed kind of annoyed because Lainie had told him he was spending too much money on lunches. He got really mad."

"Did he think the criticism was unjustified?"

"No," said Maria, snickering. "He was mad because it was Lainie telling him what to do. He couldn't stand it."

"Sour grapes."

"I guess so," agreed Maria. She looked down at a large bracelet of bright orange Bakelite that dangled on her slim wrist. She studied the bracelet and gave it a twirl, then smiled at Dewey. "I guess that's what it was." The telephone rang, and she swiveled to answer it. "Bently Foundation, this is Maria . . . Oh, hi, Hayden."

Maria's dark eyes grew wide, and she covered the mouthpiece, turning to Dewey to whisper frantically, "It's Hayden Lippincott!" She returned her attention to the call. Lippincott apparently had a great deal to say. Maria listened carefully, interposing occasionally with a sympathetic murmur.

Dewey was quite impressed with the young woman's unusual blend of savoir faire and artlessness. Maria Porter would go far in life, Dewey reflected.

"Hayden, I don't know what to tell you," Maria was saying. "There *was* a policeman here this morning, talking to Mr. Montrose. . . . Yes, he was at Lainie's place yesterday. . . . Spangle, his name is Lieutenant Spangle. But listen—you don't need to call him. He took your number down this morning, so I think he'll call you."

She listened some more; Dewey could hear a faint, tinny echo of the great actor's voice coming through the back of the telephone receiver. Maria, uttering a few more placatory noises, at last managed to end the conversation. She hung up and turned to Dewey with a smile.

"Whew! It's been like that all morning. Even if I *did* know something, Mrs. James, I don't think it would be very smart to go around blabbering. If she was murdered, then there's a murderer. If you know what I mean."

"I do indeed, Maria," replied Dewey. "The better part of valor, and so forth, and so on." She reached for a pen and fished a small, untidy-looking notebook out of her capacious handbag. "I'll tell you what, Maria. Since I'm a stranger, and what you might term an eccentric but mild-mannered old lady, and I have an alibi for the night Lainie was killed, I hope you will consider me above suspicion. I'll give you this number." She jotted Jane Duncan's telephone number hastily on a scrap of paper and handed it to Maria.

"If you have the urge to blabber, won't you call me? Or the lieutenant, of course."

"Thanks," said Maria, stuffing the paper into the pocket of her blouse.

Dewey rose. "Thank you very much for the tea, my dear. I advise you to be quite careful and circumspect in everything you do until this matter is settled. Will you promise me that?"

"Sure thing, Mrs. James."

"Good. Now—do you think that your curator might be free to show me around upstairs?"

"Marge?" Maria bounded out of her chair and opened her office door. "Sure, I don't see why not. She's not in a very good mood," said Maria, dropping her voice to a whisper. "But then, Marge is never in a very good mood."

"Well, then," said Dewey. "I suppose there's no time like the present."

12

THE SECOND FLOOR of the Bently Mansion consisted of a series of extraordinarily stately rooms, each now serving its small purpose in the furtherance of scholarship and the arts. Dewey James, leaving Maria Porter, ascended. She mounted the wide flight of richly carpeted stairs and took a left at the landing, toward the gallery, where Marge Gantry presided.

Even if that woman had not possessed a quiet, reverential air, the aura of the place would soon enough have bestowed it upon her. On the landing and along the corridor that led to the gallery, the walls were hung with monumental tapestries, depicting lush outdoor scenes. The largest of them showed a group of women strolling through a shrubbery, parasols at the ready. Looking at the heavy dresses and the uncomfortable-looking shoes that the women wore, Dewey was suddenly glad that she lived in the twentieth century. She couldn't imagine what life would be like if she had been forced to button herself daily into one of those huge, stiff costumes. The very thought of all those layers made the energetic Dewey James feel suddenly tired.

The former Bently drawing room was on the right at the front of the house. It was a bright, high-ceilinged chamber, with ornate plaster moldings and twelve-foot-high double-hung windows. The room itself was a masterpiece, its grandeur not subdued by the sectioning and modern additions that had been necessary when it was converted into an art gallery. The drawing room was wonderfully suited to its new purpose; especially, thought Dewey, for showing off the Bently Collection's marvelously clean-lined and colorful marine paintings.

There were several display walls, each half as high as the walls of the room, that jutted out at odd angles. Sunlight flowed in evenly over the tops of these short walls, from the east in the morning and from the south-facing windows at the back toward the end of the day. The collection had been hung with great care, and the flow of light from the windows at the front to the large doors at the back was uninterrupted.

On the far side of the room was a small door, which led into Marge Gantry's office. Dewey took her time crossing the room, stopping to admire some of the paintings, and pausing briefly before a glass-encased cabinet that held odds and ends of Colonial memorabilia—silver porringers, tankards, and canns; cameos, scrimshaw, and letters.

She came last to a series of miniature portraits, each with a carefully hand-lettered sign beneath it, giving the name and dates of the subject. These were the Bentlys, as they had appeared through the ages. Dewey looked at the succeeding generations, detecting with amusement the ever-greater obscurity of the family's famously receding chin. The chin had shown no sexual favoritism; it had ebbed as readily from the women's faces as from the men's. The chin's disappearance seemed to be accompanied, but not offset, by an increasing protuberance of nose and eyebrows, so that the last Bently under glass—this was Pincus Schermer Bently, IV, the philanthropist—was almost comically beetle-browed.

No one could have said that the Bentlys were an attractive family, not even in the early days when the chin had been more of a feature; the people that peered out at Dewey from the tiny frames of cloissonné or gilt were sallow-faced, morose, and afraid. With all their great wealth and importance, the Bentlys were here revealed as an unhappy and lifeless bunch. Dewey was suddenly impatient with them all.

"I'm sorry," said a voice behind Dewey, "but the gallery is not open to the public today."

Dewey turned and smiled her best beatific smile. This must be the redoubtable Marge Gantry. She was a large woman with a sallow complexion to match that of the most sunless of Bentlys; her eyes had a watery glaze, and there was nothing about her face to suggest approachability. But Dewey James had met stubborner faces before, in her time. She didn't hesitate.

"Mrs. Gantry, isn't it?" asked Dewey brightly, extending a hand to shake. "I'm Dewey James, a friend of Jane Duncan's. Just here visiting, you know, from what you might consider the boondocks, and Jane is stuck downstairs in a meeting, and as I'm *rather* at a loose end, I just thought I would take the *tiniest* little look around. You don't mind, do you?"

"Well, Mrs. James, I'm actually very busy right now." Dewey noticed that Marge Gantry was holding a proof sheet of a color photograph. "Our annual report is shipping to the printer this evening, and I still have a great deal to do. It might be better if you were to come back tomorrow, during exhibit hours."

"Oh, my," said Dewey enthusiastically. "Do you mind if I have a look?" She peered at the proof in Marge's hand. "A beautiful painting."

"It's our only Edmé Chatard," said Marge, unbending a bit. "A marine painting. Quite well known."

"Marvelous. You do have quite a collection, don't you. Well. The *other* thing I was curious about," Dewey went on, unheeding, "is your library. I'm a librarian myself— well, I no longer work full-time, of course, I'm far too ancient for that. But for many years I ran our little library in Hamilton single-handedly. And just about a year or two ago we were given the *most* remarkable rare book collection— old Horace Ridgfield's collection. You may know of it, as I gather he was rather famous.''

Marge Gantry's eyes lit up—Horace Ridgfield had indeed been famous as a book collector in the first half of the twentieth century, and he had purchased for himself one or two volumes that were quite illustrious and valuable. So Marge unbent, gave Dewey an appraising look, and led the semiretired librarian from Hamilton off to the Bently library, which occupied a large room on the other side of the house.

Dewey took the tour with good grace. It would take some time to lead the conversation around to where she wanted it. Marge Gantry needed warming up. For the most part, the books were unremarkable, meriting only the most cursory of looks; perhaps the Bentlys hadn't been great readers. There were too many "sets" of things for Dewey's taste— volumes bound in luscious calf and embossed with gold lettering on the spine, which had been left to sit silent on their shelves for decades. The Waverley Novels, Dewey noticed, looked as though they had never been touched; nor had anyone apparently attempted to read the collected works of Washington Irving. Marge Gantry clearly knew little about librarianship, but Dewey was not one to pass judgment; she listened in polite silence as Marge led her along the bookshelves, pointing out this and that.

At the far end of the library, next to an elegant marble fireplace, stood an enormous globe in a gleaming cradle of polished rosewood. The globe was at least a yard in diameter, making it far and away the largest that Dewey had ever seen. She was entranced with it, charmed by the out-of-date place names and the small inaccuracies of the cartographer. The globe, Marge told her, had been won in a bet by Pincus Schermer Bently, III, who had wagered successfully the outcome of a steeplechase that had been run in 1892. "Pincus the Third took it from the man who made it. According to legend, it was the man's pride and joy; he brought it over to the house, wept, and went away. He died the next day."

"Good heavens!" remarked Dewey. "I wonder that Mr. Bently didn't forgive the debt."

Marge shook her head. "In those days a gentleman's wager was his word. That wouldn't have done. Besides— I'm sure old Bently wanted it."

"No doubt. It's very beautiful." Dewey looked again at the remarkable sphere. She could easily see that every line and every letter had been carefully put in by hand. "Must be worth a fortune," she remarked.

"We've had an offer of nearly two hundred thousand for it," said Marge. "But of course it's not for sale. Nothing in this house is for sale."

Dewey touched the globe gently, then followed Marge Gantry to a cozy corner with two large leather armchairs. The women chatted happily about books, catalogs, and other bibliotechnical matters for a quarter of an hour. Dewey was very skilled at guiding conversations; and without too much trouble she led the discussion around to the death of Lainie Guiles. By this time Dewey was prepared to hear more scathing opinions of the late director; but Marge Gantry surprised her.

"I'm probably the only one around here who will miss her," said Marge. "And I'm not even certain why, at this point—but I will."

"You were friends?"

Marge furrowed her brow. "No, not really. Workmates. We kept each other at a distance, and we were good for each other professionally. Our departments didn't really overlap, ever, so there wasn't much call for competition. She handled the social swirl, and I take care of the artwork."

"I gather, though, that there wasn't much love lost between Lainie and the rest of the staff."

"You mean Terry."

"Well—"

"There really isn't any more staff than Terry, these days." Marge Gantry pursed her lips in thought. "Unless you count Maria, who's after all new. No, they didn't get along. In fact, I have often wondered why Terry stayed on. The job he holds isn't all that demanding—nothing to it, in fact. He wanted Lainie's job, but there was no way he was going to get it."

"Oh!" said Dewey softly. "I rather thought he had been promoted."

Marge Gantry bit her lower lip and shook her head. "He's a pushy man, no question about it, but that business of moving into her office really takes the cake."

"Will he be chosen as the new director?"

"For now, I suppose; the Bently is rather a rigidly run institution, Mrs. James, as you have probably gathered. According to the bylaws, the assistant director takes over, at least for a three-month period, to assure continuity. Old Pincus didn't want any interlopers, and this was his way of being sure that whoever is in charge is properly steeped in the Bently traditions. But Terry Fenhaden won't last in that job. Lawrence Montrose can't stand him."

"Ah," replied Dewey.

"To be honest, nobody can stand him." Marge Gantry smiled—the first smile that Dewey had seen—and looked at her watch. "I had better get back to my office, Mrs. James," she said, rising. "If you'd like to stay and look around, please be my guest."

"Thank you ever so much," Dewey replied. "I would very much like to take another look at the paintings, if you don't mind."

"Not a bit." Marge led the way back to the gallery, where Dewey spent a happy half hour admiring the paintings of the clipper ships and other types of vessels that had served the interests of commerce and pleasure along the eastern seaboard through the nineteenth century. You didn't see much of this sort of thing in Hamilton, whose commercial needs had been served by river barges and paddle-wheeled steamers through the last century.

There was a small group of illustrative paintings of the early years of the America's Cup races; Dewey didn't care for the style but was intrigued by the history. The Bentlys had owned several competing boats at the turn of the century; one of them, she read on a small plaque, had capsized, and all hands had been lost.

As she turned to leave, Dewey noticed with interest a gap on one of the far display walls. Someone must be cleaning a painting, she supposed. She stepped up and read the small plaque; the missing painting was the clipper ship *Ferdinand Plaisance*, one of the fleet belonging to the Holcombe West Indies Trade Company. No doubt this was the painting that Lucas Hanover had purchased, she realized suddenly.

She made her way back downstairs again, where the meeting of the trustees had just, evidently, broken up. There Jane Duncan once more took Dewey under her enthusiastic wing, introduced her to some of the other trustees, and shuttled her out the door into the cold December air.

Night had fallen, and as the two friends made their way to Madison Avenue for a taxi to take them home, Jane sighed heavily.

"What a business," she remarked at last as she flagged down a passing cab.

"What do you mean, Jane?" Dewey asked as they climbed in the backseat. The cab was rickety, and the suspension in the backseat had long ago given up the ghost. The driver kept a small vial of sweet-scented air freshener on his dashboard; the atmosphere was thick with the putrid odor of chemicals. Dewey rolled down her window as far as it would go—a matter of an inch or two—desperate for fresh air.

"Lexington and Ninety-third, please," Jane told the driver, who roared away from the curb and screeched through a red light. "I'll tell you later," she replied to Dewey. Then she took a deep breath and held it as they zoomed crazily north on Madison Avenue. Dewey laughed and did the same.

13

At his desk in the 16th Precinct house, Lieutenant Francis Spangle was staring hard into a small mirror. He stroked the enormous, drooping, fulvous fronds of his walrus mustache. To trim or not to trim? In his left hand he held a tiny pair of scissors; these he opened and shut, opened and shut, in his indecision.

Lieutenant Spangle had little thought what awaited him as he changed Lainie Guiles's file designation—from an "S" prefix, for suicide, to an "H" for homicide. Murder was almost a commonplace in New York, but Spangle knew well the public's taste for high-society homicide. The murder of the Bently Foundation's director was the toniest, upper-crustiest murder that New York had seen in many a year, and the story had kicked up a raging typhoon of publicity. All morning long the telephones had been ringing off the hook, and the precinct house had been swarming with reporters.

The evidence of homicide hadn't been obvious, but because he had bothered to look, Spangle was assured of a case. There were no fingerprints on the word processor where the supposed suicide note had been typed; in and of itself, this circumstance was suspicious. In addition, the wine bottle and corkscrew that had been found in the dead woman's kitchen had been wiped free of prints. Of the cork there had been no sign; the police were still searching for it, but Spangle believed that the murderer had pocketed it.

There had been nothing in Lainie Guiles's medicine cabinet answering to the description of the barbiturates that had killed her. No empty prescription bottles had been found on the premises, nor did her doctors have any record of a prescription for barbiturates.

The really telling evidence of foul play, however, came out at the autopsy. The report had just reached Spangle an hour before; the postmortem examination had revealed tiny lacerations and bruises in Lainie's throat. These, the pathologist said, showed that some kind of foreign object—perhaps a tube of some sort—had been forced down her throat. The medical examiner speculated that Lainie Guiles had been knocked out with an initial dose of the barbiturate in her wine; and that subsequent to her losing consciousness, she had been force-fed another, much more toxic dose of the stuff. Death had come after about eight to ten hours of unconsciousness.

As he stared at himself in the mirror, Francis Spangle had almost begun to wish that he hadn't answered that niggling doubt in his mind. It was too late now to go back on his decision to investigate the case further. Now the hounds of the media had arrived, Minicams at the ready. They were there, at this moment, out in the press room, baying for an interview. It was their presence that had brought Lieutenant Spangle to his present pass. For the first time in his career, Spangle was in charge of a very high-profile case. He wasn't at all sure that the mustache *worked*. It was certainly not the kind of mustache that a member of the Bently Foundation Society would sport.

In fact, while Lieutenant Spangle hated to say so, the time had come to sacrifice the mustache. Its ponderous length had begun, for the first time, to seem absurd. The time was now—before the first Minicam began to roll. Once his face appeared on the six o'clock news, there would be no going back.

The telephone on his desk rang.

"Spangle."

"Sir, did you want to talk to the press?" It was Sergeant Skinner, sounding harried.

"Not now, Skinner."

"Uh, okay. When, sir?"

"When I'm good and ready."

Spangle hung up the phone and picked up the scissors. The die was cast. He began to snip away, and the long red hairs fell softly to his desk, making a neat pile.

At six o'clock that evening Donald Brewster and Hayden Lippincott were seated on well-worn stools before the long, mirrored mahogany bar at the Old Cove Bar and Grill. There were a few other customers in the Old Cove this afternoon; mostly men, mostly well dressed, a few looking a bit worse for wear. On a television overhead a desultory talk show was going forth, with muted volume; the popular sage nodded, probed his guests, and mugged for the camera in silence, accompanied by the silver tones of Bobby Darin, whose "Beyond the Sea" blared from a jukebox in a corner.

The Old Cove was well known as a refuge for down-and-outs who had once been up-and-coming. Ball players who were past it, Wall Streeters caught in a fiddle, Madison Avenue types whose clients had shifted agencies, authors whose well had run dry, and accountants who had lost their head for numbers—all kinds came to the Old Cove of an afternoon to escape the *schadenfreude* of their former colleagues or the onus of a routine grown stale beyond all redemption.

The Old Cove didn't offer redemption. It was merely a place where it was possible, even easy, to feel unalone—to take comfort in the company of the gray-suited men and (increasingly) the well-heeled, professional-looking women who came here for solace of an afternoon.

Hayden Lippincott had once been an habitué of the Old Cove, during a particularly rough patch of his career. The bartender, Hal McKeown, was sorry to see Lippincott back in the Old Cove today, but he knew the reason for it. There had been many times, over the years, when Lippincott had spent day after day at the Old Cove, staring into a beer glass and fretting about his career or his relationship with Lainie Guiles.

As the early dark of the December evening shuttered down outside, Brewster and Lippincott ordered martinis. Lippincott remarked, with a grin, that his ambitious under-study would have a chance to strut his stuff tonight. "No way I can go on," he said.

"Not if you plan to sit here all day, drinking like a fish. I'll call the theater." Brewster set his drink down, un-touched, and started for the public phone at the rear of the tavern.

"No." Lippincott held him back with a firm arm. "I'll be all right."

"If you say so."

They sat in silence, sipping at their drinks. Finally Lippincott spoke again. "In all the drama, Donald, I'm afraid I've neglected to offer my congratulations."

Brewster gave him a blank look. He and Jane still hadn't made their engagement public. "Congratulations?"

"The Pinkie," said Lippincott. "Have you forgotten the Bently Medallion?"

"Oh." Brewster in fact *had* nearly forgotten about the Bently Medallion. It seemed an age since Lawrence Mon-trose had telephoned him with the news. Now he waved it away. "It's just a silly little award from a stuffy little group."

"I wouldn't say that." Lippincott did his best to manage a grin. "Prestige galore, and thirty thousand smackeroos. I'm your leading man, Donald. We ought to slap each other on the back."

"So we should. So we should." Brewster reached for a pretzel from a dish on the bar and munched thoughtfully. At last he seemed to find a way to speak. "I'm terribly sorry about Lainie, Hayden."

"Thanks." Lippincott finished his drink and signaled to the bartender for another.

"Seriously. If there is anything I can do for you—"

"Forget it, Donald. Just sit here and drink the afternoon away with me."

"That's hardly an answer."

"It answers for today. It answers."

Brewster studied the actor's face. It bore no signs of grief. His strong jaw was set firmly, his forehead was unfurrowed, and his eyes were clear. But, of course, Hayden Lippincott was used to controlling his facial expressions; it was second nature to him. And he was a very private person, as Brewster well knew.

There had been rumors about a split between Hayden and Lainie for months, but Brewster didn't know how much truth was in them. In theatrical circles one tended to disregard the talk about romance; so much of it was the work of the gossip columnists, or the overeager public. Hayden Lippincott, Brewster knew, had once been deeply in love with Lainie Guiles; but that had been long ago, it seemed. It was impossible to read grief in the actor's face this afternoon.

"Hayden, the police don't seem to think Lainie killed herself."

"Don't they?" Lippincott raised an eyebrow. "First I've heard of it. What do they think—that she sat utterly still while a prowler drew her a bath and slit her wrists for her?"

"I've no idea what they think. But Jane Duncan says there were plenty of detectives on the scene."

"They always send detectives."

"And that the police have spent a good deal of time questioning everyone at the foundation."

"Oh? They think someone in the office did her in?"

"Perhaps."

"Absurd."

"Isn't it more absurd to think that Lainie Guiles killed herself?"

"Wouldn't know." Lippincott was clearly feeling the effects of the second martini, which he had downed in a couple of gulps. He waved at the bartender, who brought him another. Brewster rose, somewhat unsteadily—he was unused to martinis—and went to the small room at the back of the bar, where there was a public telephone. He spoke briefly to the stage manager at the Gilman Theater and arranged for Lippincott's understudy to go on that evening.

When he returned to the bar, Hayden Lippincott was no longer alone. He had been joined by Lieutenant Francis Spangle.

Lippincott turned to Brewster with a wry grin. "The Law has arrived." He gave Spangle a long stare. "How did you find me, Officer?"

"Your agent thought you might be here."

"Oh. She talks, that one."

Having faced the Minicams for the early edition of the television news, Spangle was like a new man. He was ready for action. He had been galvanized and strengthened by his confident decision to shave his mustache; thus emboldened, he was in no mood to be put off by the rich and famous of New York. "Don't hold it against her, Lippincott," said Spangle smoothly. "I didn't give her much choice."

"No. How about a drink?" Lippincott wriggled a finger at the bartender.

"Not for me, thanks. I need to talk to you, Mr. Lippincott. I'm sure that's no surprise."

"No. Not a surprise." The bartender came and stood before them, mutely inquiring. His face was impassive, but the curiosity shone from his bright blue eyes. The Old Cove could be pretty lively, one way and another. A smart bartender learned how to listen without the appearance of listening.

"Get you gentlemen something?" he asked.

"Not for me, thank you," said Spangle. He dismissed the man with a look and returned his gaze to Lippincott.

Lippincott smiled, and then began to talk, his voice full of bonhomie. "My friend Donald and I were just talking about you fellows. You know Donald Brewster, the playwright? It's his show I'm skipping out on tonight"—Lippincott shot a wrist out and squinted at his watch—"curtain in just an hour. I'll never make it. Donald, did you call the theater?" The martinis had made Lippincott unusually talkative—or perhaps it was the presence of the police. He was certainly more garrulous than usual: his public persona.

Brewster raised an eyebrow. "Yes." He turned to Spangle. "Uh—Lieutenant, is it?"

"That's right," said Spangle with a nod, drawing up a bar stool and seating himself.

"Lieutenant," interposed Brewster, in his customary calm tone of upper-crust authority, "no doubt you are aware that Mr. Lippincott has suffered a terrible blow. Can't this wait?"

Spangle shook his head. "Afraid not. You know better than to ask me, Mr. Brewster. If you don't approve of my tactics, you are free to go. For the moment."

Brewster didn't respond, but from his attitude, and the way he sized Spangle up, it was clear he planned to wait this one out. It made little difference to Spangle, who could ask questions of his suspects just as efficiently in a bar as at the precinct house. Which is not to say, necessarily, that he was remarkably efficient in either venue—just that the time and place had little bearing on his technique.

"Mr. Lippincott," Spangle began, "is there anything you can tell me that would shed light on the occurrences of the other evening?"

"Nope." Lippincott took a sip of his drink and stared straight ahead.

Spangle pulled a small notebook from the breast pocket of his jacket. "You were performing that night, I believe."

"Every night but Monday."

"What time did you leave the theater?"

Lippincott scratched his cheek thoughtfully and shot Brewster an interrogatory glance. "Donald? How long does your play run?"

"Usually till ten-forty."

"Make it eleven, then, Lieutenant," said Lippincott, unbending slightly. "Eleven, or thereabouts."

"And what did you do after leaving the theater?"

"I went straight home. I live on the Upper East Side, not far from Lainie's apartment. I took the bus."

"Long way to go on the bus."

"Not at that hour. You'd be amazed—the forgotten network, the bus lines. Quickest thing going after nine o'clock at night."

"Mmm." Spangle was a dedicated subway rider; if he couldn't make his way quickly somewhere underground, he generally didn't bother to go. "All right. The bus got you home at—"

"About eleven-twenty-five, give or take. It's a straight shot up Third Avenue."

"Yes, I see." Spangle made a note to check the Third Avenue bus lines for the nighttime schedules. Not that the New York City bus drivers really stood much chance of adhering to their posted schedules, but it was worth a try. "What did you do then?"

"I stopped in at the vegetable market on the corner of Third and Seventy-fifth street and bought an avocado, a bag of corn chips, and a six-pack of beer. Budweiser," he added, before Spangle could ask. "Then I went home and made myself a bowl of guacamole dip and lounged on my sofa, eating it and drinking beer, until about twelve-thirty. Then I got sleepy, went to bed."

"Did you talk to anyone? Did anyone see you?"

"The doorman on duty saw me, I'm sure."

"Ah, yes. That's something I wanted to ask you about. I understand that you have a very thorough security system in place in your building."

Lippincott nodded. "We've had quite a few unpleasant incidents lately. Which, if you don't mind my saying so, the police have been rather slow to interest themselves in. As a result of this *crime wave*, Lieutenant, everyone entering the building must sign in."

"Yes. So I understood."

"So—you'll find my name right there, on that night's sign-in sheet." Lippincott was scowling again. "Now—hasn't this little bull session of ours lasted long enough? Run away and catch yourself a murderer, like a good policeman."

"I intend to do just that, sir. Thank you for your time. I'm sure I'll be seeing you again shortly." Spangle rose, gave the two men a long stare, and departed.

When Spangle had gone, Lippincott remained tense, his deep blue eyes fixed intensely on the mirror behind the bar, his grasp on his glass tightening. Ignoring Brewster's attempts at conversation, Lippincott transferred his stare to his drink. Brewster signaled to the bartender. Clearly, it was going to be a two-martini evening.

14

IN HER TINY apartment in Yorktown—just one room, but all her own!—Maria Porter stood on a chair so she could see herself better in the small mirror atop her maple dresser. Maria's salary at the Bently Foundation barely paid the rent, so she didn't have much in the way of a wardrobe. She had worn her only really good dress to the Pinkie Dinner on Thursday night; somehow she didn't think it would be right to wear the same outfit to Lainie's memorial service this afternoon. With a sigh she held up an old suit of blue wool—still intact, and very well made, but hopelessly out-of-date. Her mother had bought it for her during her first year at college. Thankfully, Maria was as slim at twenty-two as she had been at eighteen; the suit still fit. The wide lapels made her feel like a cauliflower, and the immense, thick, long skirt made her feel like an old maid. Maria sighed again. There was no help for it.

She rummaged in her small bureau drawer for something to dress the suit up with, at last managing to find a blue and white scarf with an equestrian print on it—a present from her great-aunt for graduating from boarding school. There was some kind of discoloration on one corner; Maria practiced tying the scarf about her neck until the stain was hidden. It would do. It would have to do.

Maria dressed quickly. It was cold outside, but the sun

was shining, and she thought it might be nice to walk to
work this morning. It would clear her head, which was
swimming from the events of the last few days. There had
been so many things to take care of.

The memorial service was scheduled for two o'clock at
St. Stephen's Church, on Seventy-fourth Street and Park
Avenue. This bastion of the socioreligious establishment in
New York had seen its share of high-profile weddings,
high-society baptisms, and interesting funerals. The vestry
staff were accustomed to coping with crowds and reporters;
the Church Altar Guild knew well how to do the flowers
nicely for these semiprivate occasions. The memorial service for Lainie Guiles, therefore, posed no problem except
for that of space; for while actual mourners were not
abundant, the prominence of the Bently Foundation, and the
nature of the director's sudden and malefic death, guaran-
teed an enormous crush of curious New Yorkers.

Maria had learned, in the last few days, to handle the
reporters easily enough; this task was simplified by the fact
that she was as much in the dark as everyone else about the
progress of the case. It was definitely a case now. Lieutenant Spangle and Sergeant Skinner had become familiar
figures at the foundation. They had interviewed everyone at
least twice, including Maria; they had taken away the
carbon duplicates of her telephone log, and they had warned
everyone who worked at the Bently not to leave town.

The local newspapers had carried the story on the front
page for three days. The articles were accompanied by
photographs of the Bently Mansion, and an old portrait of
Pincus Schermer Bently, IV. The reporters predictably
made much of the social angle—well, thought Maria, you
couldn't really blame them. If she hadn't herself been at the
heart of the maelstrom, she would undoubtedly have found
the murder first-class entertainment.

But she was at the heart of it; and Maria had to admit that
she was frightened. Lieutenant Spangle had questioned her
again and again about Lainie's personal life; now, the longer

she thought about it, the more deeply she was convinced that there were few people who had known Lainie Guiles well enough to wish her dead. Despite Lainie's wide acquaintance—the result of her position at the Bently—she hadn't had many friends or close associates. Unfortunately, of those few, nearly every one of them was connected in some way with the Bently Foundation—all but Hayden Lippincott. And if the last few months had been typical, probably all of them *had* wished her dead, at some point or other. In her abbreviated life Lainie Guiles had not bothered much about friendship.

Lainie would be buried in Indiana, where she had been raised, and where her father—with whom she had not been on speaking terms for the last six or seven years—had saved her a place in the family plot. She was, after all, his only child. Maria had risen bravely to the task of helping with those arrangements; she was not a squeamish young woman, but practical. And she felt rather sorry for Arnold Guiles. How sharper than a serpent's tooth, and all that.

Maria tugged on her thin tweed coat, bundled a scarf about her neck, and headed out for the office. It was a beautiful day.

In his small but influential art gallery, on the third floor of the old Meyerson Mansion on Madison Avenue, Lucas Hanover was leaning back easily in a comfortable leather chair, a broad smile on his handsome face.

"We did it, Susanna," he remarked to his partner.

Susanna Christiansen laughed, a long, loud, merry laugh, her blue eyes sparkling with mischief. "Who said the Bently Collection couldn't be sold?"

"That's right. Who said so?"

Hanover had every reason to feel pleased with himself. This morning he had received payment in full from his buyer for the painting of the clipper ship *Ferdinand Plaisance*. Even when the purchase price from the Bently was deducted, the margin was considerable. More than considerable.

The Chatard painting was generally regarded, by experts in the subject, as the finest of its genre. The buyer was a monomaniacal collector with nothing better to do than be parted from large chunks of his considerable fortune. Accordingly, Lucas Hanover had satisfied all parties. He happily contemplated the check. After taxes, and a percentage for Susanna, there would still be enough left over to put his small son through four years at Columbia University. Not bad, for a day's work.

"Terrible about that woman," remarked Susanna Christiansen, making a note in the leather-bound calendar on her desk.

"Lainie Guiles. I know." Hanover scratched his head. "She's the one who helped me set up this deal. I was going to take her to dinner at L'Avarre when the money came through." He looked at his watch. "There's a service for her today at St. Stephen's. I think I'd like to go."

"You should go," concurred Susanna.

"I guess I'll put the cost of dinner at L'Avarre in the plate, if they pass it."

"They'll faint," said Susanna.

"Who? The clergy at St. Stephen's?" Hanover shook his head merrily. "They're used to it. They'll probably think it's peanuts."

In the days since Lainie Guiles's death, Terry Fenhaden had settled himself comfortably into her office. He loved the feeling of the famous Windsor chair, loved the view out the window onto Seventy-third Street, loved the massive walnut desk and the cherry bookshelves that lined the walls. By Tuesday morning he had begun to feel that the mantle of authority was finally his own.

His own! And yet he was only thirty-five years old—well, nearly thirty-six. But what a remarkable achievement it was for him! At last he had what he had wanted for ten years—the directorship of the Bently Foundation.

Last night Terry Fenhaden had carefully read through the bylaws of the foundation. By their terms any director pro tem was assured of the position for three months. Even if the trustees replaced him in the spring, Terry Fenhaden felt that his future was golden; as a former director of the Bently Foundation, he would carry quite a bit of weight. Any nonprofit organization worth its salt would be lucky to have him.

He had planned to spend the morning basking in this success; but his pleasant reveries were disturbed by the arrival of Lawrence Montrose. Fenhaden and Montrose had never been on good terms, not even in the best of times, and now the young director pro tem steeled himself for an unpleasant confrontation. But he had the bylaws on his side. He felt confident.

"I don't care what you thought, Fenhaden," Lawrence Montrose was saying. His voice was icy, but beyond the repugnance apparent in his manner and his face, he betrayed no emotion as he stood before Fenhaden. Montrose picked up a paperweight—a smooth brass oblong, which had been a present to the Bently from a former Pinkie winner—and looked at it idly. "I want you, and all your things, out of Lainie's office by five o'clock."

Terry Fenhaden, his face suffused with red, glared at Montrose. "You haven't got the authority, Larry."

"You know damn well I have the authority to do whatever I please at the Bently Foundation. This office is not up for grabs, Terry."

"Oh, no?"

"No. And, by the way, I've called a staff meeting for this afternoon. Before Lainie's service."

"Skeleton crew, Lawrence." Fenhaden chuckled dryly.

"Bad taste, Fenhaden." He put down the paperweight with a menacingly quiet gesture and looked levelly at Fenhaden. The younger man's eyes flickered momentarily with wariness. "Shall we say one-fifteen, in the dining room?"

"I can't imagine what there is to discuss." Fenhaden folded his arms, and a stubborn look appeared on his sallow face. "In fact, the bylaws clearly state that I'm the one who should be calling the staff meetings. Why don't you pick up a copy of the rule book, Lawrence? And while you're at it, remember that I'll also be the one deciding who gets invited to those meetings. And who gets chosen to sit on the Bently Medallion Selection Committee. So if you think you have your own little empire sewn up, Lawrence, just remember that I'm not playing by your rules any longer."

Lawrence Montrose's eyes narrowed, and the tip of his snub nose began to redden. Beneath the fabric of his handmade Italian suit, the muscles in his shoulders rippled. When he spoke, however, his voice was as smooth as silk.

"Watch your step, Terry. You're not as clever as you think." Montrose headed for the door and turned to offer a parting shot. "Not clever enough, by half. Don't try to take me on. You're not a match for me, Terry."

Montrose departed, and Fenhaden rolled his eyes. Then he turned to some files on his desk and began to sort idly through them. It was high time that he began to consider his new duties. With evident relish he picked up a folder marked CONFIDENTIAL. He pushed back his shirtsleeves and began to read.

After fifteen minutes he reached for the telephone book, found the number he wanted, and dialed.

"Hello, Donald? Terry Fenhaden here, from the Bently. Yes, yes. That's right, it is this afternoon. Listen, Donald—there was something I wanted to talk to you about. Have you got a moment? Good, good. It's about your play, *The Latter-Day Don Juan.*"

15

On Tuesday afternoon Dewey and Jane had lunch at the Stilton Club, an imposing edifice on Park Avenue where rich ladies met and mingled and (as far as Dewey could tell) congratulated themselves for being themselves. This kind of thing wasn't Dewey's cup of tea at all; it wasn't really Jane Duncan's, either, but she had been raised in it, and it was unrealistic to expect that she not feel, at some level, the urge to take part. The female members of Jane's family had been Stilton members for four generations.

"You'll love it, Dewey, I promise," Jane told her. "It goes against every egalitarian bone in your body, I'm sure, but you mustn't sit in judgment."

Feeling dismally provincial in her plum-colored woolen dress, Dewey swallowed her objections. All she really wanted to do was to spend the afternoon at a museum or taking in a Broadway matinee. But she quashed her desires and put on her lipstick and gamely accompanied her friend to the tiled elegance of the Stilton Club for what promised to be a rather dull lunch hour.

In the end Dewey was glad she had gone. They had a third for lunch, Lily Feldspar, an old friend of Jane's who had been until recently the director of community relations at the Bently Foundation. The three women, naturally, had found a rich vein of conversational material in the recent goings-on at the Bently Foundation.

Lily Feldspar was about the same age as Jane and Dewey. An impressively tall woman, with blond hair only now beginning to show white in places, she was full of energy and enthusiasm. Dewey listened quietly as Lily told Jane about her last weeks at the Bently.

"Jane, I tell you, there is something fishy about that place."

"Please, Lily, for heaven's sake, don't tell me that. I've just finished promising a huge endowment to Lawrence Montrose."

"I think Lawrence is all right. Although you never know, do you? But that Lainie Guiles was trouble from the day she walked in the door."

"Lily, are you sure this isn't just sour grapes talking?"

Lily Feldspar shook her head, causing an enormous faux-pearl necklace about her throat to rattle massively. "Not sour grapes. I was on the point of handing in my resignation anyway, although it sounds lame to say so, and I would never tell anyone else—but I can trust you to believe me."

"All right, Lily," said Jane. "I believe you." Jane looked at Dewey. "And so does Dewey. I can tell, by the way that she's playing with her shrimp cocktail, that you have caught her interest."

Dewey laughed and reddened slightly. "Jane knows better than most what an inquisitive old busybody I am. She likes to tease me about it, but I deserve to be teased, I suppose."

"You do deserve it, Dewey," Jane concurred, breaking a breadstick with a loud snap. "But seriously, now, Lily. Tell us. Because you know, one way and another, my life is becoming utterly bound up with those people."

"It most certainly is, Jane." Lily fixed Jane with a long stare. "I don't suppose your Donald has offered any insight?"

Jane shook her head. "When he was nominated for the Pinkie, I forbade him to discuss the Bently with me. It seemed the only reasonable course of action. Things being how they are," she added with a shy smile.

"I'm glad to hear you've been so honorable. I suppose you know as well as I do what gossip in this town can do."

"Surely," put in Dewey with a tentative air, "Jane isn't the subject of gossip?"

"Naturally she is," responded Lily Feldspar. "Not as much as she might like, given the right circumstances, but people are interested. They are definitely talking." She let out a hearty laugh.

"Oh, hush, Lily," insisted Jane. "Or—don't hush, but tell us something we don't already know."

"All right, then. I will." Lily Feldspar leaned in across the smooth white linen tablecloth, taking in both of her interlocutors with a conspiratorial glance. "I think there was something odd going on at the Bently."

"Odd? Odd as in—what?" Jane was still refusing to bite.

"Dewey, forgive me if I go on and on about people you don't know. Jane, you know that greasy little man who writes for the *Clarion Call*? Homer Brown's nephew, the one who kept trying to marry Pristine Nearing."

"Garrett Brown?" asked Dewey, who as met with a look of surprise. "Well," she explained, "Maria pointed him out to me at the Pinkie Dinner the other night."

"Goodness," said Lily Feldspar. "Jane did *not* exaggerate. You are perceptive, Dewey." Her eyes had a sudden wariness.

"That's a nice word for it," said Dewey with a smile.

"You mustn't mind Dewey," said Jane. "She was always this way. She just remembers about people and things. It comes in very useful from time to time, I believe."

"I can't help myself," added Dewey.

Lily Feldspar gave Dewey a long, careful look. Then she resumed her story.

Shortly before Lily's unceremonious departure from the

Bently Foundation, she told them, she had been approached by Garrett Brown, who had told her he wanted to do a story on the foundation for *Nine Muses*, a small arts journal. He asked her for an interview. As luck would have it, Lily Feldspar was acquainted with the man who published the journal, and, happening to mention the article to him at a dinner party the following evening, was dismayed to learn that Garrett Brown had fed her a line. *Nine Muses* was planning to publish no such story by Garrett Brown. In fact, Lily's friend told her, he doubted that Garrett Brown even knew how to write. All he seemed to know how to do was to drop names.

"Good heavens, Lily!" said Jane Duncan. "What did you do?"

"I naturally did what anyone might have done, Jane. I played along with the little pup. He had scheduled the interview for the next day, which was a Wednesday. Wednesdays are usually slow at the Bently, because it's not a Public Day, and I had plenty of time on my hands.

"So I let him come along, as we had planned, and I gave him a tour of the foundation, and I made him suffer through an impenetrable lecture on the history of the Bently family, not neglecting to tell him about Lobelia Bently, who had been nearly thrown in jail for perjury in 1875. He didn't turn a hair, just kept taking notes and saying inspired things like 'How very interesting, Mrs. Feldspar.' Then I took him upstairs to the collection and introduced him to Marge Gantry, who bent his ear for half an hour or so."

"Was Marge in on the secret?"

Lily Feldspar shook her head firmly. "Not on your life. Well—you know how sensitive Marge can be. I thought she might consider that a practical joke had no place in the Bently Foundation. Besides"—Lily Feldspar's eyes lit up with mischief—"it was a *far* greater punishment for that young man to have to listen to the provenance of every painting in the place. You know how Marge goes on."

"I do, indeed," said Jane, nodding.

By this point in the story Dewey James had completely
overcome her apprehensions about the lunch hour; and she
was halfway to revising her opinion of stuffy ladies' lunch
clubs.

"Did he ever catch on?" she asked.

Lily Feldspar shook her head. "No. That is—I certainly
never told him. He came downstairs from the tour with
Marge and came back into my office, and I gave him
another history lesson. Of course what he was after was
information about the management of the place; he kept
dropping in little questions about grants, and funding, and
oversight of financial matters. But in my years of sitting on
boards and so forth I have learned very well how to talk at
great length to no purpose at all." She laughed gently.
"And so I bored him to tears and sent him away."

"Nicely done, Lily," Jane congratulated her. "But what
on earth do you think he can have been after?"

"Besides a free lunch? Who knows?" Lily Feldspar
shrugged her shoulders. "But here's where it gets intrigu-
ing, Jane. The next day I was in a meeting with Lainie
Guiles, Marge Gantry, and Lawrence Montrose. We were
going over some of the articles for the annual report, and
Marge mentioned Garrett Brown's visit. Well! Suddenly
there was so much tension in the air that you could have cut
it with a knife."

"You mean Lainie didn't see him when he was there?"

Lily Feldspar shook her head. "She was out of town,
drumming up money in Philadelphia or somewhere. No, not
Philadelphia. Bridgehampton. The Steinbergs."

"Why do you think she reacted the way she did?"

"I don't know. I tried to ask her about it, very casually,
the next day. But I got nowhere. And the day after *that*,
Jane, she gave me my walking papers. And the next thing
you know, she's been murdered."

"Good gracious!" exclaimed Jane. "But, Lily, surely
you don't think—"

"I don't know *what* to think, Jane. Perhaps your friend

Dewey can do our thinking for us while we order coffee. Dessert, anyone?''

"No, thank you," replied Dewey in an abstracted tone. "Jane—here's a question for you. What do you think that young man was doing at the Pinkie Dinner?"

"Good question, Dewey," commended Lily Feldspar. "He certainly wasn't on any list that I ever saw."

"No? And yet there he was, large as life," said Jane Duncan.

"Larger," said Lily Feldspar. Which was ungenerous, perhaps, but the truth.

"Well," said Jane firmly, with a look at her watch. "We had better get moving, Lily, if we expect to be in time for that service. I'm sure the church will be just as crowded as it can be. Dewey is going off to a museum or something, I believe." She glanced questioningly at her friend, who gave her a thoughtful look in response.

"Do you know, Jane dear," said Dewey slowly, "I rather think I might like to pay my respects. Do you think anyone will object to my coming along?"

"Good heavens, no," answered Lily Feldspar. "The whole damn city will be there. Which is funny, you know, because Lainie Guiles really didn't have any friends."

"Pity," commented Jane.

"No," said Lily. "Just the way of the world. Shall we, ladies?"

The service for Lainie Guiles was very well attended. It was short and sweet—much sweeter than Lainie had been, if the things Dewey had heard about the murdered woman were true. Lawrence Montrose gave the eulogy, talking comfortably about Lainie's many contributions to the community, her dedication to the work of struggling artists, and the loss felt by all who had known her. Everyone listened politely enough; and while Montrose spoke, Dewey James, seated in a middle pew with Jane Duncan and Lily Feldspar, contemplated the crowd.

There were several familiar faces there; everyone from the foundation, of course, as well as the Pinkie Selectors with whom she had dined. Donald Brewster had been asked, by Hayden Lippincott, to help with the seating and organization. "In the absence of pallbearers," Lippincott had said.

Dewey reflected that Brewster, in a dark suit with a boutonniere, must be feeling a bit like a hired mourner out of Victorian England. But perhaps he didn't mind so much. He had, after all, known Lainie fairly well. On the other hand, Jane had told Dewey that Donald had never understood what had drawn his friend Hayden Lippincott to Lainie Guiles in the first place; and that the woman had caused the actor nothing but unhappiness. Still, Dewey didn't suppose Brewster was disposed to demur.

She did her best to feel that the whole thing wasn't a show in hypocrisy; but as much as she was always prepared to take people on their merits, Dewey found the presence in the front pew of a smirking Terry Fenhaden almost too much to bear.

After the service Dewey stood on the church steps with Jane, scouting the crowd. She spotted Lieutenant Spangle easily enough—he was conspicuous in spite of the curtailment of the rather remarkable mustache he had sported the first time Dewey had met him. As she watched him sizing up the mourners, distinguishing those who had known Lainie Guiles from those who had merely come to gape or—worse—to see and be seen, Dewey felt a stab of pity for the police detective. He really did stick out like the proverbial sore thumb; but perhaps this didn't bother him. On the other hand she could imagine that the Bently Foundation crowd, and all their hangers-on, could close ranks fairly swiftly and effectively if they chose.

Dewey reconsidered the point Jane had raised last week. She supposed her old friend was right, in a way; Dewey James was in a better position, with regard to the people involved, than was Francis Spangle. Certainly Lily Feldspar wouldn't have volunteered to him—nor to any detective—

the peculiar events of Garrett Brown's visit to the Bently; but there at lunch at the Stilton Club, she had evidently felt she could talk to Dewey James. Which was peculiar, when you thought of it, because Dewey was a perfect stranger, and every inch an outsider. But because she was Jane Duncan's friend, and Jane's guest at the Stilton Club, Lily Feldspar had opened right up. Dewey wondered briefly if she ought to bring the story to the detective's attention.

Perhaps, after all, this was what Lily Feldspar had had in mind.

The bright-eyed librarian from Hamilton considered the point. Jane Duncan had accused Lily Feldspar of venting spleen. Jane and Lily had been friends for many years; therefore it was interesting, and perhaps telling, that Jane hadn't been prepared to accept, on first blush, Lily's tale of strange goings-on at the Bently Foundation.

There was Lieutenant Spangle, right there, talking to no one in particular and looking just the tiniest bit out of his element.

Perhaps, after all, it might do some good.

Dewey gathered her coat about her and made her way through the milling crowd of mourners.

"Good afternoon, Lieutenant."

"Ah. Mrs. James." Spangle nodded distractedly, quickly returning his gaze to the crowd.

"I wondered if I might have a word or two with you."

"About anything in particular, ma'am?"

"Well," said Dewey, feeling hesitant, "yes. That is, about the case. How it's progressing, and so forth."

Spangle laid a large, heavy hand on Dewey's shoulder and looked her in the eyes. "Just fine, Mrs. James, thank you."

"Well, you see, I noticed that you were here at the memorial service, and I know that police detectives do go to funerals and memorial services, and so forth, if the case isn't solved." She gave him a bright smile. "And I did think, perhaps, that I might have some information that could be helpful.''

"Do you, now?" Uh-oh, thought Spangle. The police captain in her hometown had been right, no doubt about it. She was definitely the amateur-detecting type. Time to take things in hand—before this dizzy dame spun out of control.

Spangle put on the face that they taught in the community relations course at the Police Academy. "Mrs. James, I know that you mean well, but I'm afraid that we can't allow speculation from outsiders to cloud our judgment in a case like this. I don't mean any offense, you know, but you are, really, a stranger in town. And I sincerely doubt that there's anything you could tell us that we don't already know.''

Dewey saw a familiar stubborn look make its way across Francis Spangle's face. "You've shaved your mustache," she replied.

Spangle looked uneasy. "I have."

"I like the new look, very much," said Dewey.

"Well, that's very nice of you to notice, ma'am."

Dewey was gratified. "Well, the thing *is*, Lieutenant, that I do have a habit of noticing things. I don't know why, really; it's kind of built in. I'm a librarian—perhaps you didn't know that—and I have often felt that it helps to have a noticing kind of eye. In my work, I mean."

"Yes, ma'am."

"I certainly don't want you to think me intrusive, Lieutenant."

"No, ma'am."

"On the other hand, if I had noticed one or two odd things about the people involved in this case, and I then failed to point them out to you, wouldn't you consider that I had been somehow lax in my duty as a conscientious visitor to your city? At the very least you might wonder how I managed to run the Hamilton Free Library for thirty-some years, if I weren't sensitive to things and of a noticing disposition.''

Spangle had been trying very hard not to laugh; but at last

Dewey's wide-eyed persistence had got the better of him. He permitted himself a low chuckle. "Okay, Mrs. James, out with it." His eyes sparkled.

"Well," said Dewey in a near-whisper, "to begin with. Behind me, if you look over my left shoulder, you will see a man. He's about five-feet-ten, close to two hundred pounds, with stringy brown hair and greasy wire-rimmed glasses. He's wearing a very dirty old trenchcoat."

"I see him," Spangle whispered back.

"Good. Now—his name is Garrett Brown. He's an investigative reporter, and I just know that he's after something. A story on the Bently Foundation."

"Is he, now? Well, Mrs. James, I don't suppose he'd be much of an investigative reporter if he weren't after a story. Am I right?"

"Yes," said Dewey firmly. "Sophistry aside, however, Lieutenant, I have it on very good authority that he was digging something up on the Bently Foundation. I have no idea what it was, exactly, but I am fairly sure that he was interested in what he felt might be some kind of wrong-doing."

"Well, now we've got a story for him, complete with a dead body. I would betcha, Mrs. James—if we permitted gaming here in the City of New York—that your reporter has gotten himself all worked up by the murder angle by this point. No flies on him. Might even get a scoop." He laughed along with Dewey at this small witticism, then tugged at the cuffs of his jacket and strode manfully away.

Dewey, watching him go, reflected that policemen were very much the same the world around.

She caught sight of Jane Duncan waiting for her at the curb. Jane had managed to flag down a passing taxi (Jane had always had a lucky knack for this kind of thing); she stood, holding the door open and searching the crowd impatiently. Dewey waved and hurried to meet her.

"Where on earth is Donald?" Jane complained.

"I saw him just a second ago inside the church. Talking to that dreadful young man from the Bently."

"Terence Fenhaden? I wonder why on earth?" Jane shook her head firmly.

"Lady!" shouted the taxi driver, through the open back door. "You want to go somewhere?"

"Oh, hush," said Jane. "Start your meter if you like, sir, but I will not be bullied."

The taxi driver, by way of response, reached back over the seat and slammed the door shut. Then he took off with a mad squeal, straight into the path of an oncoming car. There was a huge noise of brakes, accompanied by shouting and honking. Dewey gritted her teeth, but Jane Duncan didn't even appear to notice. It was just the way things happened in New York City.

16

On Wednesday Dewey James was determined to pry herself loose from the swirl of events surrounding the Bently Foundation. After long consultation with Jane over breakfast, she took herself off on a voyage of exploration. She had spent Monday afternoon admiring the newly restored beauties of the New York Public Library—she had gone from a sense of duty but had lingered a long time, enthralled by the rediscovered elegance of the place. Today, however, she hoped to have a more intimate adventure. She was headed for the Susan Dixon Library, a highly regarded and very specialized institution in Midtown, not far from Rockefeller Center and just a stone's throw from Brooks Brothers, where she planned to buy a small present for her good friend George Farnham. One thing was certain about her hometown of Hamilton: It didn't offer much in the way of men's clothing stores.

The Susan Dixon Library had been founded in the mid-nineteenth century by a woman whose great desire for learning had found itself nearly eclipsed by the constant demands of her large and noisy family. Susan Dixon had inherited a modest townhouse from her great-aunt, and in its comfortable rooms she had established a retreat and sanctuary of erudition for herself and many of her women friends.

In those days the library had been called "The Female Scholars' Room"; it was open only to women (only to gentlewomen, in fact), and it had been a source, Dewey knew, of great comfort to generations of respectable women who had needed not only the facilities of a library but also the peace and quiet of a place removed from domestic tumult.

In those days, women who joined the Female Scholars' Room had been sworn to absolute secrecy—there were quite a few husbands and fathers, in those dark times, who had considered the habit of study in the weaker sex to be a form of indecent rebellion. One woman, according to legend, had been confined to her house for six years after her husband had learned that she had been spending her afternoons reading Homer. Fortunately, her sisters in crime had been able to smuggle books to her on occasion.

Gradually the ossified barriers to women's education had crumbled, and in consequence the Female Scholars' Room had been transformed from an afternoon cloister into an enchanting little private library. As the collection grew, the custodians had chosen to emphasize American arts and letters; as a result, the Dixon Library had a very fine and rather important collection of the novels, plays, and poetry written in the United States during the nineteenth and twentieth centuries. Although men were now permitted to join, and secrecy was no longer a requirement, the place still had about it the air of a safe haven—far from ringing telephones and the intrusions of business and the everyday world. It was still, very much, a universe apart from the cacophony and the aggression of the city outside its walls.

Dewey had walked to the Dixon Library from Jane Duncan's house, and by the time she reached Forty-ninth Street, she was exhausted. It was not the walking that tired her—at home in Hamilton, Dewey rode nearly every day and spent many hours in other kinds of vigorous exertion. But she was wrung out by the noise of New York, so unfamiliar and so relentless; and by the strangely confrontational nature of every exchange. Even the small act of crossing the street, she found, required an inner reserve of determination—sometimes even of contentiousness. As she made her way south along the narrow, crowded sidewalk of Madison Avenue, she wondered how on earth Jane Duncan had survived in New York for so long. It seemed to Dewey that the crowds and the noise would eventually be too much for even the toughest of natures.

As Dewey made her way thankfully into the dark and tranquil library building, she half expected to find the place full of female scholars in long dresses and bustles. The ground floor, however, was nearly deserted; the only person present was a large man with the face of a bassett hound and a tiny gray-and-white goatee that stuck out like a piece of cotton wool on the soft promontory that jutted out between his fleshy jowls. Dewey exchanged a few polite words with him and asked if she might have a look around; he assented and returned to his book, stroking idly at the hairs of his tiny beard.

Dewey spent a happy half hour reading the names painted onto the wooden plaques that lined one of the walls. During the first few years there had only been a handful of members in the little secret society of erudition—three Dixon women and two others. Dewey, reading the names, concluded that the others were Susan Dixon's cousins, or perhaps her sisters. But the renegade idea had apparently been swift to catch on; within fifteen years of its founding, the Female Scholars' Room was a second home to more than fifty women. And by 1868 the group had been forced to purchase a much larger plaque on which to enter their names.

In 1885, Dewey saw, there had come a turning point. Apparently the need for secrecy had vanished; Dewey read, on a small caption adjoining the plaque for that year, that the Female Scholars' Society (as it now openly proclaimed itself) had held a public auction of artworks in order to raise the money necessary to send Susan Dixon's youngest grand-daughter, Emily, to Bryn Mawr College. Dewey smiled. She was thankful to these women, who had braved the anger of their husbands and the disapprobation of society in order to improve themselves and the future generations.

Still full of thoughts of women in bustles, Dewey made her way up a narrow staircase to the second floor, where the rare books and first editions were on display. Upstairs she was surprised, and a bit dismayed, to find that the modern century had intruded itself—for the first thing that met her eye was a small computer, off in a far corner, its screen aglow with bright yellow letters.

Dewey was intrigued. By her calculations, the Dixon Library only held about seven thousand volumes—a tiny number, in the world of libraries. So Dewey was surprised to find that the people running the library had bothered to install a computer system. Surely, research in the open stacks was just a question of browsing until you found something that caught your interest. The place was chiefly suited to be a kind of elaborate reading room.

But a computer, she knew, was now considered *de rigueur*. Back at home in Hamilton, Dewey had recently witnessed her own little library being swept along in the modern electronic tide. The Hamilton Free Library, at the insistence of the new librarian, Tom Campbell, had put its card catalog on a computer; but Dewey, who frankly and frequently admitted to being an old-fashioned sort of librarian, used the old index-card system out of stubborn preference. In return for her stubbornness, she came under a constant barrage of teasing attacks and snide remarks from Campbell, the young man whom she had hired when she had cut back on her own workweek. Tom Campbell, alas, had turned out to be a rather repellent person; but librarians were rare in Dewey's part of the world, so he stayed on.

Dewey knew that Campbell was secretly glad of her ignorance of the computer system. It gave him superiority, at least in one respect. Dewey didn't even know how to turn the computer on; and thus for six or seven months it had lurked and winked at her in her precious library while she cast about for the time, or perhaps the courage, to learn how to use it.

But here was an opportunity! Dewey was a great believer in kismet. She looked carefully at the machine. It was the same brand that they had in Hamilton, but Dewey was uncertain whether this fact was meaningful. Still, it might be amusing to have a go at it. And if the Susan Dixon Library had taken up the torch of electronic information retrieval (the very locutions made Dewey shudder!), then perhaps it was time for her to get down off her high horse. She glanced over her shoulder to be certain there were no witnesses to her apostasy; then she sat down before the computer and followed the simple instructions on the screen.

In short order, Dewey was transfixed. The Dixon computer system had a record of every book and pamphlet in the place and notes about some that were not even in the collection. She began idly to search through the computer's memory, entering names as they popped into her mind and cruising about through the web of the computer's mind, looking up an author here, a title there.

She was amused to see that the subject index of Domestic Economy included comparatively few titles; probably the antidomestic fervor of the library's founder had permeated the minds of all those who had come later. Most of the books in the library were literary works; a very few were political in nature, and there were a handful of biographies of important American women. Susan Dixon's great-granddaughter, Jean, had written the definitive book on Mary Todd Lincoln; its importance was signaled by the presence of two copies in the library's collection.

Dewey was interested to see how easy it was for the computer to provide very complete information on each book or subject. In some cases, the librarians had evidently added their own highly idiosyncratic appraisal of the material in question—it was like having capsule reviews ready to hand. And after each title and number, a code appeared on the screen, giving the name of the person or institution that had borrowed the material.

Dewey, following the directions on the screen, pressed a function key. That was easy enough! she thought. Then, as the screen instructed, she entered the name of an author: Brewster, Donald. In an instant a list of all of Donald's published plays came up: six in all. She noted that *The Latter-Day Don Juan* had been checked out to Lainie Guiles at the Bently Foundation—probably in connection with Donald's nomination for the Pinkie.

This computer business really was easy, Dewey admitted to herself. And if she were forced to be absolutely honest, it was rather a lot of fun, once you got the hang of the thing. Poor old Tom Campbell would be terribly disappointed if he thought his electronic supremacy would be challenged by Dewey's sudden facility on the computer system; she resolved firmly not to show off her new knowledge when she got home to Hamilton.

Deciding that she had daydreamed long enough before the mesmerizing screen, Dewey took a short tour of the stacks and display cases and finally departed. On her way out she stopped at the front desk to tell the goateed custodian about the copy of the play that Lainie Guiles had taken out. Dewey James knew how irksome such disappearances could be for the staff of a library. Then, feeling altogether adventurous, she headed to a restaurant next to the public skating rink at Rockefeller Center. There, after a prolonged (and stunned) perusal of the menu and its prices, she treated herself to a cappuccino (four dollars!). Watching the skaters go around and around, she sipped slowly at the warm, foamy drink. Before long she had forgotten all about shopping at Brooks Brothers for a present for George Farnham. There was something else on her mind.

Ten minutes later Dewey presented herself once more to the goateed man behind the desk at the Dixon Library.

"I'm terribly sorry to disturb you," she said politely,

noting the reluctance with which he put down his book to look at her. "The thing is, I'm a librarian myself, visiting from out of town, and I have one or two questions about the computer system that you are using."

"What's that?"

"Well, I was fascinated, absolutely fascinated, to see that when a book is checked out, the computer notes the name of the person who borrowed it. Is there a cross-file?"

The fat man scratched his beard and looked at her. "Madam, I can't just go around giving out information."

"Oh! dear me, of course not. No, I wouldn't *dream* of prying into the private affairs of your library." She smiled. "I only work part-time these days anyway, my hours have been cut back so *dreadfully*, you know. And I'm afraid that I shan't be able to keep up. I'm rather awkwardly placed, you see." Dewey launched into a description of her mythic struggles to learn to use the new computer in the Hamilton Free Library. She was rather hard on the hapless Tom Campbell in the process; after all, he had committed no crime except that of having a repellent personality. But her description of her predicament, if largely untrue, was efficacious. The goateed man slowly unfolded from his armchair and followed her up the stairs.

Within a moment or two Dewey had the information she was looking for. Lainie Guiles had checked out another book. It was another play, by an unknown author, called *The Runabout*. It had been privately printed about seventy years ago.

Dewey, under the pretense of practicing, called up the entire file on Lainie Guiles. It was most interesting, indeed; especially when she compared the titles to the list of Bently Medallion winners for the last five years. Lainie Guiles had been brushing up, no doubt. No doubt.

When she had her facts in hand, Dewey was impatient to be gone; but the man with the goatee, once started on his project, seemed to want to lead her down all the possible paths of computer literacy. With great difficulty Dewey extricated herself. She had, indeed, learned a great deal. Whether or not she would be able to put her knowledge to any useful purpose remained to be seen.

17

"WELL, I'M CERTAIN *I* don't know what's wrong with him," said Jane Duncan plaintively. She and Dewey were having a cocktail in her living room; they were dressed for the theater (Jane had got them tickets to *Les Misérables*), but they had been waiting half an hour for Donald Brewster to turn up. He had just now called to say he was very sorry, that he wouldn't be able to make it to the show with them. "I've had the most miserable day. I wish he would understand and be supportive. But all he can think about is that *he's* upset. About who *knows* what."

"Jane, if you think Donald is upset for some reason, we can always skip the play. Or I can go by myself." Dewey was concerned.

"Don't be ridiculous, Dewey. Of course I mean to find out what's bothering Donald, but that can wait. You haven't been to New York in ten years at least, and all I do is involve you in one criminal episode after another, and drag you around to murder scenes and funerals."

Dewey suddenly remembered the way Donald Brewster had looked on Tuesday afternoon at Lainie's memorial service—pale and shaken. "Do you think he's just upset about Lainie?"

"We're *all* upset about Lainie," Jane pointed out. "It was a terrible thing. I hardly knew the woman, but murder

140

strikes at the heart, Dewey dear. It's a dreadfully *frightening* thing, when one *knows* the person.''

"You're absolutely right, Jane.'' Dewey grew thoughtful, and Jane Duncan began to stir uncomfortably.

"But you needn't point out to me, Dewey, that Donald was more upset than you or I might have thought he would be. I could see that.''

"Yes.''

"Don't you think, though, that perhaps he's dreadfully worried about Hayden?'' Jane's voice had regained its hopeful tone.

"Hayden?'' Dewey shook her head. "I know they're close friends, Jane.''

"Well, *yes*, Dewey. Hayden is a very sensitive man, and he and Donald are quite close.''

"Well, perhaps you're right, Jane.''

"I do wish that police detective of yours would find the man who murdered Lainie.''

"He's not *my* detective at all, Jane. If he's anybody's, he's yours.''

"Yes.'' Jane sighed. "You're always right about everything. Dewey—listen. Let's forget all about going to a show tonight, and go and talk to Lieutenant Dingle.''

"Spangle.''

"Spangle.''

"I don't think he really cares to hear from us, Jane. I tried to talk to him on Tuesday, I really did. But he was most dismissive.''

"Ooh! Dewey—you've been holding out on me. You have a *clue*, don't you?''

"Not at all, Jane.'' Dewey shook her head firmly. "I merely had an idea about something, that's all. It was quite a small idea, really, and Lieutenant Spangle made me see that.''

"No, it wasn't small. It was probably the one clue they need, Dewey, and they ignored your advice, and now they'll never get to the bottom of it, and there will be a murderer on the loose for the next seventy years." As Jane Duncan delivered this speech, her voice rose higher and higher. She was nearly breathless when she reached the end; she looked at Dewey wide-eyed, and suddenly the two old friends began to laugh.

They laughed for a long time, indeed, in the way that only the very best of friends can laugh together. Each time that Jane managed to catch her breath, she caught Dewey's sparkling blue eyes as well. Then the two friends would collapse in a renewed fit of giggles.

"Seventy years!" exclaimed Dewey at last, when she could manage to get any words out at all.

"At least seventy." Jane smoothed down the skirt of her dark blue silk dress. "Perhaps eighty. Dewey, you simply must get to the bottom of all of this. Why is Donald so upset? What was Garret Brown after? And who, oh, who, murdered Lainie Guiles?"

"And why," added Dewey thoughtfully, "did Lily Feldspar lose her job?"

"What?"

"Well, don't you see, Jane? It goes straight to the heart of the matter. Straight."

"I don't see it at all," complained Jane, with a willing hopefulness in her voice. Evidently she would very much like to see—whatever it was.

"Jane, do you think perhaps your friend Lily would like a last-minute invitation to the theater?"

Jane's eyes twinkled. She rose and hurried toward the front hall, where the telephone stood guard on a small table. "You know, Dewey, I just think she might. Lily adores the theater. Shall I call her?"

Lily Feldspar did indeed adore the theater. But, she told Jane, she had seen *Les Misérables* not once but three times.

"Jane, I just couldn't bear that heartbreak again. Not tonight. I have a better idea, anyway. What about the new

Broadway Out of Bounds? I hear that Carla Aldrich is back in the show.''

Jane and Dewey had a hurried consultation on the matter, and in short order they were on their way to the cozy supper club on the West Side where *Broadway Out of Bounds*, an acclaimed send-up of the musical stage, had been playing off and on for ten years.

Over a light dinner the three ladiés were deeply amused by the parody of all that was lame-brained, show-offy, and inane in the musical theater. Dewey, although familiar with only about half the shows being satirized, was gratified by the choice, because the dinner-theater setting enabled her to grill Lily Feldspar between the song-and-dance numbers.

Lily Feldspar was one of those perpetually eager people whose energy seemed destined to outrun their intelligence. She was a forthright woman, with a good sense of style and well-honed conversational skills—all attributes that had made her the perfect ''front man'' for the Bently Foundation. Dewey thought it odd that the foundation should have let her go after so many years in the public relations spotlight; and she said so.

Lily Feldspar nodded in agreement. ''Well, Dewey, as I mentioned the other day when we were lunching at the Stilton, I was really ready to get on with my life anyhow. Jane thinks that's sour grapes, but it's not, I swear it.''

''I believe you,'' said Dewey. ''It interested me, you see, that Lawrence Montrose should have let you go so suddenly. And, as Jane will tell you, I'm an incurable busybody.''

''And why not?'' asked Lily Feldspar. ''Nobody ever got anywhere minding their own business.''

Dewey wasn't altogether sure she agreed with this sentiment; but she had to admit to herself that in her case, at least, it was true. True enough, anyway. ''Well, Lily, then I hope you won't mind if I ask you one or two questions.''

''Go right ahead.''

"When Garrett Brown came to see you, did he discuss the painting collection with you at all?"

Lily Feldspar shook her head. "If you remember, I sent him upstairs to talk to Marge Gantry."

"You didn't hear their conversation?"

"No. Not at all."

"But you said that Marge was the one who mentioned Brown's visit in the staff meeting the next day."

"That's right. Marge brought it up—but naturally, I was the one who had opened the door to him. I think that Lawrence Montrose felt it was a dangerous thing to do."

"But naturally, you had never felt, until that time, that there was any problem with the Bently?"

"Good gracious, no. Since the death of the last Bently, the family escutcheon hasn't had a smudge—not a smudge." Lily Feldspar laughed at her small joke. "That is, nobody thought it did."

"How much do you know, Lily, about the awarding of the Bently Medallion?"

"Oh." Lily Feldspar looked uncomfortably toward Jane. Dewey understood the meaning of Lily's glance. "Don't worry about Jane. She won't take any of this to heart."

"Yes, but—it's all most fearfully hush-hush, you know, Dewey."

"Yes, I'm aware of that. I'm also thinking, don't you know, that secrecy is a great breeding ground for things of a dark nature. Sometimes even of a criminal nature."

Lily Feldspar reached for her wineglass, took a swift gulp, and began to talk. The secret rituals of the Pinkie Selection Committee, it appeared, were well known to her, although she had never been a member of the committee. Once—just once—she had lingered at the foundation building after the Selectors had arrived; secreting herself in the butler's pantry, she had observed the whole bizarre transaction.

"It doesn't really add up to anything. They all wear ridiculous getups, and drink far too much, and quarrel among themselves. When everyone is thoroughly sick of everyone else, they all stand up and spout something in Latin; I think it might be from the *Aeneid*, but it's a long time since my school days. And nobody seemed to understand what it meant anyway. Then they cast their votes.''

"Did it seem to you that there was any possibility of vote-fixing?''

Lily Feldspar shook her head. "It did occur to me, however, that there were two people who exerted a great deal of control over the proceedings.''

"Which two?''

"Lawrence Montrose and Andrea Follet.''

Jane Duncan, who had been thus far paying minimal attention to the conversation, perked up immediately. "You mean to say that Andrea Follet is a Selector?''

"Naturally. She has been for years.''

"That's odd,'' said Jane.

"What's odd, Jane dear?'' Dewey prodded, fearing that she knew the answer.

"Donald told me that she had paid him a visit. On the night that the Selectors were meeting.''

"Well, obviously he had the wrong night,'' said Lily Feldspar.

"Oh, no. We laughed about it quite a bit, you know. Because Donald had long been convinced that Andrea was on the committee. When he let it slip that he'd had a drink with her, I quite naturally pressed him for details.'' Jane colored slightly. She turned to Lily Feldspar. "Dewey and I went to the theater that night, you see, and we had wanted Donald to come with us, but he said he wanted to spend the evening quietly, at home. Well.'' She sighed loudly and shook her head. "I am only human, after all, and Donald is my intended. Naturally I asked about it.''

"It was *quite* natural to ask, under the circumstances,'' said Dewey, trying to bolster Jane's feelings. "What did he tell you?''

"Oh, nothing much. That they'd had a drink, I suppose.

And I said that obviously if Andrea Follet was bending her elbow with him, she couldn't very well be a Pinkie Selector.''

"And what did Donald say to that?" prodded Dewey.

"You know, it's funny. He didn't answer me, really—or we changed the subject. And we really haven't talked about it since then." She regarded her friend closely. "Dewey."

"Yes, Jane?"

"I can tell you think Donald has something to do with all of this. Don't you?"

Dewey was silent for a moment. Then she looked Jane right in the eye. "I'm afraid, my dear, that Donald is indeed involved, one way and another. But let's just take this one step at a time, shall we? There's no need to panic," she added, seeing the terror creep into her old friend's face.

Dewey was wrong, at least, about the panic issue. The Bently Foundation was about to be swamped by a tidal wave of problems. Everyone aboard would soon panic.

18

ON THURSDAY MORNING, Lucas Hanover paced in the foyer at the Bently Mansion. Gone was the good humor for which he was so well known in the New York art world; his face, this morning, was a study in anger.

Maria Porter, having made an effort to exchange polite greetings, had meekly retreated to her small office, leaving the famous dealer to walk impatiently up and down the black-and-white marble floor. It was ten-fifteen; he had been waiting on the front stoop when Maria opened the mansion's great front door at nine-thirty.

Lucas Hanover had called to see Marge Gantry, who had lately become something of an enigma. She had been out most of last week, and Monday as well, with the flu; on Tuesday afternoon she had made an appearance at the memorial service for Lainie Guiles, avoiding everyone from the foundation and disappearing as soon as the service was concluded. Such behavior was, to say the least, out of character for Marge, who quietly prided herself on her dedication to her work and the late hours that she habitually kept. Maria Porter secretly thought that Marge worked late to avoid her husband, a self-important entertainment lawyer with too much time on his hands and too few influential friends. Lainie Guiles, never a nice person at the best of times, had liked to snicker about Marge's husband, calling him short and greasy (which he undoubtedly was, on the evidence) and a prig (Maria had no evidence, one way or another, of his priggishness).

Whether or not Marge's dedication to work stemmed from loathing of her husband, Maria felt that at some level it was genuine. Alone of them all, Marge Gantry really seemed to care about the Bently Foundation. The rest of them—Lainie, and Terry, and Lawrence Montrose, and even (Maria was forced to be honest) Maria herself—were in it for what they could get out of it. Marge, however, seemed to cluck and brood over her collection like a hen with a prize egg on the nest. It was unlike her to miss a single day of work; and in three years (Terry Fenhaden had said), Marge Gantry hadn't been out sick once.

Lucas Hanover knocked at the door to Maria's office. "Excuse me, Maria. I know none of this is your problem—but would you mind trying Marge's number again? I simply have to talk to her. Also—do you expect Montrose to come by today?"

"I don't know about Mr. Montrose. He usually drops in once or twice a week, but I—well, I don't know if he'll continue to do that. I can call him at his office downtown, if you want."

"Thank you. Tell him that I need to see him as soon as possible."

"Sure thing." Maria, thinking that the Bently Foundation was becoming an increasingly weird place, did as she was asked. There was still no answer at Marge's house, and Lawrence Montrose's secretary merely said she'd have him return the call if it was convenient.

Terry Fenhaden turned up for work while Maria was making her calls. She heard Hanover follow him into his office and shut the door; and even through the thick walls, she thought she could hear a heated exchange going forth. Maria's big dark eyes grew very wide indeed. She had the distinct feeling that there was scandal brewing.

* * *

"I don't care who knew it or who didn't, Fenhaden," said Lucas Hanover evenly. After a brief outburst he had regained his cool. Now he was comfortably ensconced in the leather chesterfield in the late Lainie Guiles's office, one knee crossed casually over the other. He examined his fingernails with a distracted air and resumed. "We're left with one fact: The painting that the Bently Foundation sold me is a forgery."

Terry Fenhaden swallowed hard. "Are you sure about this, Lucas?"

"Don't be an idiot. Or at least, Terry, don't be more of an idiot than you already are. The fake is a good one, I'll admit—but it wasn't intended to fool anyone for very long. You have got one colossal mess on your hands now, Fenhaden."

"But I don't understand how this could have happened."

"I don't give a damn how it happened. The bottom line, Fenhaden, is this: My buyer called me this morning because he had hired Sharon Bates to make a new frame for the thing. The framer—the *framer!*—was the one who discovered the forgery."

"You trust the word of your framer about something like this?"

Hanover laughed bitterly. "Sure. It doesn't take a Ph.D. in art history to see the words *Made in Taiwan* stamped on the back of the canvas."

"What do you mean, Taiwan?"

"The canvas that the thing was painted on was fabricated, Terry, on the perfumed island of Formosa. Probably as recently as last year."

"Maybe Chatard always got his canvas from Taiwan." Even to Terry Fenhaden, uninstructed in history and art alike, this suggestion sounded rather silly.

"Right," said Hanover. "Right. Listen, Fenhaden, my buyer is very upset. And he's not upset with the Bently Foundation—oh, no. He doesn't give a damn about the

Bently. But me, *me* he's upset with. Thinks I tried to sell him a bill of goods, and now he's setting about to ruin me.''

"Well, surely, Lucas, you can explain—"

"Explain to Richard Basson?"

"Oh." Fenhaden's face crumpled like a fallen popover. Richard Basson was, at the moment, probably the most famous man in New York. He was a self-made millionaire (real estate, lumber, and concrete) whose tastes, until lately, had run to flashy yachts and tacky women. But all of a sudden, about three years before, Richard Basson had begun to effect a dramatic and very public transformation—from "rich boob to rich, high-falutin' boob," as one of the wags had put it. Suddenly, as though someone had given him a crash course in discernment, he had begun to turn up on important boards, at places like the Metropolitan Museum of Art, and at dinner parties in the homes of exceedingly particular New Yorkers. He had even, at the age of thirty-seven, taken up polo—someone had explained to him that polo was in extremely good taste.

For Richard Basson—and indeed for legions of deep-pocketed social climbers in Manhattan—the purchase of expensive works of art was one of the necessary steps to acceptance; as though, moving their game pieces avidly around the board, they had at last landed on the square that bade them "Buy Five Modern Masters and Roll Again." To buy bad art, or the wrong art, was a mistake; to purchase a forgery, displaying the credulity of the truly unenlightened, was a disaster. Such a gross error, if it became public, would humiliate Basson, who was not known to pull his punches.

Suddenly Terry Fenhaden understood the urgency of the situation.

"I didn't realize Basson was your buyer."

"Now you know." Hanover glared. "I know he's an idiot, but he's a billionaire ten times over, and for the past three years he has been a very good customer. I worked very hard to sell him that Edmé Chatard, which God knows he didn't need. So I expect not only that the foundation will discover the original for me, and deliver it to me in perfect condition, but also that the foundation will issue a full and very public apology for the laxity of its curatorship.''

The blood had drained from Terry Fenhaden's face. He had worked so hard, had covered every possible angle, and finally all the pieces were falling into place for him. He had waited ten years for this directorship—and now it appeared he would preside over a disintegrating institution that was destined to be the laughingstock of the city.

Hanover seemed to read his mind. ''You wanted this job, Terry. Now you've got it.'' He rose and donned his soft cashmere coat. ''When I was a greedy little boy, my Chinese nanny used to warn me: Be careful what you wish for—you might just get it.''

Hanover departed, leaving Terry Fenhaden in stunned silence. He sat, dumbstruck, for a full three or four minutes before he rallied. He had regained his bullying tone.

''Maria!''

Maria Porter appeared in the door, a small scowl on her smooth, pale forehead. ''Yes, Terry?'' For the third or fourth time this week, she contemplated looking for a new job. It had been one thing to be the assistant to Lainie Guiles. Working for Terry Fenhaden was another kettle of fish altogether; fairly stinky fish, from what Maria could judge.

''Get me Marge.''

''I've been trying all morning. Not home.''

''I said get her. You'll do it now.''

Maria rolled her eyes and bounced away, shaking her head. Something was definitely up. She dialed the number once more. This time, Marge answered.

''Hi, Marge. It's me, Maria Porter, at work. At the Bently.''

''Oh.'' Marge sounded doubtful, as though unsure of who Maria Porter might be, or indeed what the Bently was. ''Yes?''

"I'm *really* sorry to bother you at home when you don't feel well. It's just that Terry says he needs to talk to you."

"Oh."

"So if you'll just hang on a minute, I'll put him on. Okay?"

"Sure, Maria. Sure. Thanks."

Maria buzzed Terry Fenhaden on the intercom, and he picked up the line.

Never in her life had Maria Porter been a snoop. She had never sneaked a peek at her little sister's diary, nor peered through a keyhole or a crack in the door to try to see something that was off-limits. But this morning, as Terry Fenhaden took the call, Maria's blood began to run cold. Obviously something terrible was going on here, and Maria was scared. Moreover, she was indignant, feeling more like a pawn than ever. She had a right to know what was going on. The blood rushed to her face and pounded in her ears. With a shaky hand Maria Porter gently lifted the telephone receiver.

"—about it. If you weren't the one, Marge, then who?" Terry Fenhaden's voice had an urgent quality to it that Maria had never heard before.

"Leave me alone, Terry. I don't know what you're talking about. I have the flu and I feel awful. We'll talk about your problem some other time."

"This is *your* problem, Marge," he said venomously. "Your mess. You made it, now you clean it up."

"Terry—"

"Or I'm going to make sure that everyone in the world hears about this. Do you understand me?"

"Terry, this kind of thing happens all the time." Marge had evidently begun to rally. "Remember those Egyptian cats at the Gotham?"

"Nobody tried to sell those cats, Marge."

"Terry, I should be feeling better by Monday. We can look into it then."

"Monday, hell. Lucas Hanover wants an answer. You'll

look into it as of now, Marge, or I'll know the reason why.''

Maria had heard enough. She put the receiver down gently and sat utterly still for a moment, trying to catch her breath. *She* remembered ''those Egyptian cats at the Gotham'' with perfect clarity. It had only been six months since the scandal broke. The Egyptian cats were bronze statues, and the pride of the Gotham Museum's antiquities collection for more than a century. But six months ago the bronze cats had been revealed as fakes—elegant forgeries that had convinced learned authorities for a hundred years.

That conversation could only mean one thing, Maria realized. The painting by Edmé Chatard of the clipper ship *Ferdinand Plaisance* had been a fake.

Maria Porter sat lost in thought for a few moments. No *wonder* Lucas Hanover had looked so steamed! Terry Fenhaden was going to be in pretty deep over this one; and Maria wasn't at all sure that she wanted to stick around to take the heat.

She rummaged in her handbag and came out with a small scrap of paper that bore a telephone number. She reached once more for the telephone and dialed.

''Good heavens, Jane,'' said Dewey James when she had hung up the telephone.

''What *is* it, Dewey?'' asked Jane, her eyes wide. She had been avidly hanging on to every word of Dewey's end of the telephone conversation for a good ten minutes, and she was clearly bursting with curiosity.

''Jane, do you recall Lily Feldspar's tale of the corpulent reporter?''

''That *ghastly* Garrett Brown. Of course I do. He's the one that lost Lily her job.''

''Well, do you know, Jane, he may have been on to something.''

''You're not serious?''

''Perfectly serious. Maria—well, I shouldn't tell you quite everything—''

"Don't be ridiculous, Dewey." Jane was affronted.

"I'm not being ridiculous. Jane—Lucas Hanover bought a painting from the Bently, didn't he?"

"Well, *yes*. That Edmé Chatard of some boat or other. I never much cared for it myself, although it was always said to be very fine."

"It turns out, according to Maria, that it was a forgery."

"You're joking!"

"No, I'm not. I am most assuredly not joking." She related the gist of Maria's tale, omitting to mention that Maria Porter had listened in on Terry's telephone call to Marge Gantry. That would be revealed on a strict "need-to-know" basis, thought Dewey.

"Dear heaven, Dewey. I had better reconsider my gift to those people. And the sooner I resign my trusteeship, the better."

"I agree with you there, Jane. But—do you think you could wait just a bit longer?"

"Of course, Dewey. If you like." Jane Duncan's eyes twinkled. "You think this all has something to do with Lainie Guiles's murder, don't you?"

"Naturally," responded Dewey. "Don't you?" Without giving Jane time to answer, Dewey went on. "I've invited Maria Porter to come by here this afternoon for lunch. I hope you don't mind."

"Mind?" asked Jane Duncan. "Of course not. I'll have Sandra set another place, that's all. If it's not beneath her dignity."

Sandra Gossage was Jane Duncan's housekeeper and sometime cook—a sallow, po-faced woman in her early forties, who insisted that the aroma of cooking food turned her stomach. Sandra was a fairly good housekeeper, however—she appeared to be honest, and she knew how to keep the place tidy enough. Above all, Sandra Gossage seemed inclined to stick around. Jane therefore was loath to let her go merely on account of this one little failing in the kitchen; so Sandra was prevailed upon to make lunch for

Jane only about once or twice a month. Breakfast and dinner, of course, were out of the question. "I wonder what she's got for us today, anyway?"

"She ordered food in from the delicatessen around the corner," Dewey replied with a smile. "I saw the delivery boy when I went out to get the newspaper."

"How very like her," said Jane, heading for the kitchen.

As Terry Fenhaden had predicted, the news was soon all over town that the Bently Foundation had sold a forgery to Lucas Hanover. The buyer, Richard Basson, was much given to calling press conferences; and since anyone in possession of upward of ten billion dollars was generally considered newsworthy, the press could be depended upon to come *en masse* to his little convocations.

Basson held a press conference at noon, in the lobby of one of his hotels. Within minutes the story had broken onto the public consciousness, bringing gleeful snickers in the art world—a fraternity not widely recognized for its system of support and bigheartedness. Lucas Hanover's telephone began to ring at twelve-fifteen, and by one o'clock he had unplugged it and locked his gallery door.

His partner, Susanna Christiansen, crept about very quietly, trying hard to be inconspicuous. Hanover was a shrewd man and aware of the fact that all publicity is considered, on some level, to be good publicity. But just the day before yesterday he had been riding high. Susanna, for one, had never for a moment doubted the genuineness of the article in question. Now her partner's career was perilously close to extinction; and, in all likelihood, she would be out of business herself within a week or so. At two o'clock she crept out of the gallery and headed for a coffee shop down the street, where she spent the afternoon making a few discreet telephone calls.

There were naturally those who believed that Hanover had been nobody's dupe—that he had cheerfully passed along the forgery and merrily pocketed the difference. It wasn't unheard of for unscrupulous dealers to do such a thing; Hanover, it was said, would wait a few judicious months or years before offering the painting for sale on the quiet, to a collector whose thirst for a particular work outweighed his concerns about its provenance. Such things happened all the time.

Lieutenant Francis Spangle was one of the skeptics, and by the end of the day he had brought Hanover into the precinct house for some preliminary questioning.

19

"YOU HAVE TO admit, Mr. Hanover, that it all seems kind of underhanded." Spangle was leaning perilously back in the wooden armchair behind his desk, his arms locked behind his head, his jacket hanging loosely open. His face was unreadable.

Hanover tugged at the crease of his trousers and seemed to collect his thoughts.

"That is to say, Mr. Hanover," Spangle went on, "that you purchased this painting, in the first place, without the approval of the curator. At least, that's what I'm getting here. That right?"

"Yes," Hanover agreed, wondering if he ought to call in his lawyer. "Yes, that's right, Lieutenant."

"In fact, the person who authorized the sale and purchase of the work of art was the dead woman. Interesting coincidence, wouldn't you say?"

"I wouldn't care to speculate, Lieutenant."

"In fact, it's highly suspect, that coincidence."

Hanover permitted himself a small smile. "Murder is always suspect, isn't it?"

Spangle rose from behind his desk and began to pace in the narrow space between the filing cabinet and the door. As he paced, he stroked the spot where the long, drooping ends of his mustache had been; the gesture, without the facial hair

157

to make sense of it, seemed ludicrous and just a bit affected. The result was to give Lucas Hanover the impression that he was dealing with a buffoonish sort of policeman. This was a wrong impression, and a dangerous one for a person being questioned by Francis Spangle.

After a minute or two of pacing, Spangle fixed his deep blue eyes on Hanover. "Tell me when you first knew that the painting was a forgery, Mr. Hanover. If you please." He leaned his tall, bulky frame against the front of the desk and looked down at the discomfited Hanover, who began to feel that the room had grown uncommonly hot.

Hanover loosened his necktie a sixteenth of an inch and took a deep breath. "I found out from Sharon Bates this morning, sir."

"Sharon Bates being the woman who was replacing the frame?"

"That's right."

"How long have you been in the business of buying and selling works of art?"

"Fifteen years."

"Fifteen. Have you always been self-employed?"

Hanover shook his head. "I worked for the Gilpin Galleries for three years."

"Down on Fifty-seventh Street."

"That's correct." Hanover knew that he must sound like a perfect idiot. The Gilpin Galleries were the best of the best, the cream of the crop. People who worked at the Gilpin Galleries were expected to be able to recognize forgeries, at the very least.

"You attended college somewhere?"

Hanover nodded. He was beginning to feel annoyed. Spangle was trying to rile him, that much was clear. "And I have a doctorate in art history as well, Lieutenant. So if you want me to say that I should have known better, consider it said."

"What I don't understand, sir," Spangle went on, as

though Hanover hadn't spoken, "is why no safeguards were taken to be certain the painting was genuine."

Hanover shifted in his chair. "Lieutenant, if you had spent three years trying to buy a painting from the Louvre, and they had at last offered you the *Mona Lisa* at a discount, would you begin to ask questions?"

"I'm not an art dealer."

"But you must understand—that painting is famous. Chatard only painted a few canvases in his lifetime—twenty or thirty—and most of them were portraits and still lifes. A marine painting of such high quality, by someone who ordinarily opted for something quite different—well, you see, it was a treasure. The whole world knew that the Bently Foundation would never part with it."

"And yet the Bently did part with it. Did you say you got the thing at a discount? Surely *that* fact might have sounded some kind of alarm bell. Might have tipped you off." He turned and made a note on a pad of paper.

Hanover had miscalculated. Spangle had been paying attention after all. "Not actually at a discount, Lieutenant," he protested with mild suavity. "That wasn't the right way to present the deal—forgive me. Of course, I purchased the painting at a fair price, based on the free market value of marine paintings. Nineteenth-century clipper-ship paintings, in particular."

"But not the value of that painting, *in particular*."

"Well, no. I have to admit that I did pretty well by them, but the Bently got a whopping sum, nonetheless. After all, Lieutenant, whatever the margin may have been, I'm the one who found the buyer for it."

"And what a buyer." Spangle frowned. "A man made of money, eager to impress, and—this is the really important part—notorious for his lack of taste and his faulty education in what you might consider the basics, the rudiments, of aesthetics. Richard Basson made his money in concrete. He didn't even finish high school."

Hanover cleared his throat. "Education isn't necessarily the key to taste in art, Lieutenant."

Spangle chuckled. "You're right, there, Hanover. But after all, this *is* Richard Basson we're talking about. King of the bimbo-hunters. The guy who tore down the Bootles Building to open up a sports bar with a wide-screen television set and ex-cheerleaders for waitresses."

Hanover winced. Richard Basson's philistinism was legendary; there was no getting around it. Hanover supposed that if you examined the situation from Spangle's point of view, Basson looked more and more like a sitting duck. The perfect mark for a high-class swindle.

"Isn't it a fact, Mr. Hanover"—Spangle consulted some notes—"that you advised Basson against putting a new frame around the painting?"

"Yes, but that was to preserve the integrity of the whole. Of the—the package."

"No doubt."

"Listen, Lieutenant. It's true that I thought the nineteenth-century frame should stay. I was afraid that Basson would do something entirely inappropriate. But he insisted, and I finally sent him to the woman who does all of our work for us. Because I wanted him to have the best. If I had known that painting was a forgery, I never would have sent Basson to see Sharon Bates."

"I can't say what you might have done or might not have done, Mr. Hanover."

"Then I guess you'll have to take my word for it."

"No, sir." Spangle shook his head ponderously. "That's just what Richard Basson did. And look where it got him."

"Touché." Hanover tried out a smile, found that it didn't work, and scowled instead.

"When was the last time you examined the painting, Mr. Hanover?"

Lucas Hanover scratched his cheek in thought. "Probably about two weeks ago. I had a meeting with Lainie Guiles to talk about the details of the deal. She and I met in her office, then went upstairs to the Bently Collection to have a look.''

''First making sure that Marge Gantry was safely out of the office?''

Hanover thought. ''You know, Marge *wasn't* there. It didn't strike me as odd, at the time.''

''No? But this was such an important deal.''

''Well, I knew how she would be feeling about it. She's extremely protective.''

''All the more reason for her to take part.''

''Not necessarily. She's kind of odd, Lieutenant. And she usually stays put in that dark little office of hers anyway. I probably just assumed that she didn't want any part of it.''

''You were aware of her feelings on the subject of selling anything from the collection, then?''

''Sure. Hell, everyone in town knew how Marge would feel about a sale. I thought it must all be a bitter pill, and all that, but it didn't occur to me that she wasn't even in the picture. Now that I know that Lainie never even told her about the sale—well, the situation takes on a different light altogether.''

''How closely did you look at the painting at that time?''

''The paint was dry, if that's what you mean.'' Hanover chuckled.

Spangle scowled. ''If I were you, Mr. Hanover, I would refrain from making jokes. They might be misconstrued.''

Chastened, Hanover nodded. ''You're absolutely right, Lieutenant. All right: I studied it fairly closely. But I was buying a known quantity, not a pig in a poke. So I didn't give it a thorough going-over.''

''What were you looking at it for, then?''

''Just to see about the condition of it—whether it needed to be cleaned, how the frame looked, and so forth.''

''By this time your deal with Basson was fairly far along?''

Hanover nodded. "He was just waiting for their go-ahead."

Spangle nodded. "And when you took delivery of the painting?"

"It was wrapped."

"You didn't open it? Look at it? This famous treasure that you had scored from the Bently?"

Hanover shook his head. "Basson was in a rush, by now. He wanted the new frame ready by the end of the week, because he was having some fancy-dancy people for dinner, and he thought it would impress them. Cornelius and Roberta Van den Hoot," Hanover added, for effect. In New York's highest social strata, the Van den Hoots clocked in just this side of the seraphim.

"When did you pick it up?"

"On the day of the Pinkie Dinner. I stopped by the Bently Mansion on my way to the dinner, actually, and picked up the painting. Lainie had told me where it would be. I dropped it off at my own gallery and went on to the dinner."

"Who knew about this arrangement?"

Hanover swallowed hard. "The only one that I can say, for certain, is Lainie Guiles."

"No one else?"

"Lainie told me that the trustees had approved the sale. I don't know how detailed their approval system is, though—"

"You never asked about Marge Gantry?"

"I didn't know at the time," Hanover protested, "that Lainie had kept her curator in the dark."

"Hmm." Spangle stroked his whiskerless chin once more. "I'm going to let you go home tonight, Mr. Hanover."

Hanover sat perfectly still. Was it possible that he was now a suspect in Lainie's murder? He had a sinking feeling that he had moved straight to the top of Lieutenant Spangle's list.

"I'll probably want to talk to you again in the morning, however," Spangle went on. "So do me a favor. Don't try anything stupid."

"No, sir. I won't."

20

JANE DUNCAN'S TELEPHONE, like that of Lucas Hanover's, had begun to ring off the wall as soon as the scandal about the Chatard painting broke. Maria had finally arrived at one-fifteen, full of apologies for being late. While Jane talked at length on the telephone, Maria and Dewey took refuge in Jane's kitchen, which was the one spot (Dewey assured her) that they would not be forced to endure the baleful glower of Sandra Gossage, Jane's reluctant cook. They tucked in to the treats that Sandra had ordered up from the delicatessen at the corner, and Maria told Dewey about all the events of the morning.

"You know, Mrs. James, I just think all this stuff is incredibly *weird* and *scary*," Maria said. "Right after I talked to you, we got a call from some reporter at the *Chronicle* who started to ask all these questions—and it didn't stop all morning long. Terry Fenhaden started to yell at me at eleven o'clock, and he didn't let up. So I cleared out. I hope Mrs. Duncan doesn't mind."

"You did exactly the right thing, my dear," said Dewey. "I'm becoming convinced that the Bently Foundation is not an altogether worthy spot."

"Hah!" snorted Maria. "Danny always *told* me it was a nest of vipers. He works for *Gotham Arts in Review*, so I guess he ought to know."

164

"Is your Mr. Parker a writer as well?" asked Dewey politely, remembering the good-looking young man with the hooded eyes who had been Maria's date for the Pinkie Dinner.

"Well, not right now. Right now he's just a fact checker. But the magazine's editor told him that he might be able to write some things for their 'New York in a Nutshell' column, starting in February."

"Well, then, he must be extremely good at his job."

"He is," said Maria with a shy, proud smile. "But he's not like that Garrett Brown. *That* guy's a muckraker. But who would have thought there would be any muck to rake at the Bently Foundation? I should never have taken that job."

"On the other hand, my dear, if you hadn't, you would never have met that theater producer at the Pinkie Dinner. Has he had a chance to read your play?"

"Oh! Eric Brody. *Yes.* He isn't going to produce it or anything, but he wants to send it up to Andrea Follet at Hencope College. So that's pretty cool. If she likes you, you can be pretty sure that a workshop or something might pick you up."

"Is that so?" Dewey was intrigued. Andrea Follet hadn't struck her as a figure who cut a wide swath—Dewey had thought of her more as a friendly academic with a good sense of humor.

"Yup. She doesn't act like a big-deal power broker, but Danny says she's got the whole of Broadway in her hip pocket. Everybody but Howard Horde, and everybody knows he's an old drunk anyway, so that doesn't matter much."

"I see."

"Anyway, Mrs. James—"

"Maria, dear, I think we are well on our way to being friends. And, that being the case, I would very much like you to call me Dewey."

"Okay. Dewey." Maria grinned. "I think maybe we

should turn on the news. I have the feeling that this whole stink about the painting is going to be big. *Very* big. Three networks called the Bently this morning while I was trying to get out the door.''

Dewey obliged by switching on a small television set that sat atop a pile of telephone books in a neglected corner of Jane's kitchen. The picture flickered on, and Dewey and Maria were greeted with the sight of Lawrence Montrose before his office building in Midtown, politely staving off a swarm of reporters. He was smiling handsomely into the camera, shaking his head; he had a smile on his face that seemed at once apologetic and superior.

''The Bently Foundation is offering no comment, at this time, except to say that obviously this whole affair is most disturbing. Especially in light of the very real tragedy that has so recently befallen our stout little band.'' He shook his head. ''I suggest, however, that we might hope the vigilant forces of the law will take a very firm hand when they find the culprit.''

''Mr. Montrose!'' shouted a diligent reporter at the head of the swarm. ''Do you agree with the police view that the forgery and the murder are related?''

Montrose raised an eyebrow. ''I haven't heard that the police have advanced such a theory.''

''Do you agree?'' persisted the reporter.

''Well,'' said Montrose smoothly, ''I will say this much. That two felonies, coming back to back at a place as—as *untouched* as the Bently must be a very strange coincidence, indeed, if it is a coincidence. Now, if you'll excuse me, I have an appointment.'' He darted elegantly away and leapt into the back of a waiting limousine.

''What do you think of that?'' asked Maria.

''I don't know,'' replied Dewey, her tone thoughtful. ''Maria, dear—''

''Personally, I think the whole outfit is nuts. Might be good material for a play some day, though.''

"Yes, indeed. Maria, I know you don't particularly relish the idea of returning to your post this afternoon."

"Hah!" proclaimed Maria. "That's putting it politely. If I never see Terry Fenhaden again, it'll be too soon."

"I imagine you must feel that way. Still, I wonder if it wouldn't be a smart idea to have someone looking after the place."

"So no more thieves break in and forge and steal our paintings. Right." Maria laughed.

"No," said Dewey gently. "So that we can keep an eye on something. Would you like to help out?"

When Maria had gone back to the Bently, her head swimming with Dewey's instructions, Jane emerged from the small den off the living room where she had been taking telephone calls.

"I tell you, Dewey, this is just terrible. That was Lawrence on the phone. He's calling an emergency meeting of the trustees for this afternoon. Oh! I'm so dreadfully sorry. We haven't had the chance to do a single thing since you got here."

"I'm having a marvelous visit, Jane, don't you worry."

"What happened to Maria? Did Sandra's idea of lunch scare her off?"

"No. I thought, under the circumstances, that it might be a good idea to have an ally on the premises."

"Dewey, you think Donald has something to do with all of this, don't you? Don't spare me. The wedding's not till tomorrow, after all," she said, laughing as her eyes filled with tears. "It's not too late to call the whole thing off."

Dewey, struggling for an answer, was saved by the loud ringing of the front doorbell. Jane went to the door and came back to the living room, triumphant, a moment or two later. Lieutenant Francis Spangle was a few steps behind her.

"Dewey, the mountain has come to Mohammed."

"Yes, indeed. Good afternoon, Lieutenant." Dewey smiled politely. "I'm sure you have some questions for

Mrs. Duncan about all this painting business, so I'll just make myself scarce.''

Spangle cleared his throat. "No need, Mrs. James. You stay put. This won't take a minute, really.''

Dewey James needed no encouragement. Jane Duncan offered the detective a seat, and he was soon launched on an interrogatory excursion.

"You seem to me, Mrs. Duncan, if you'll pardon my pointing it out, to be more or less of a safe bet, murder-wise. Mrs. James here can alibi you for what we believe to have been the time of the murder. About one A.M.—an hour or so after the Twinkie Dinner.''

"Pinkie,'' corrected Dewey automatically.

"Right. Pinkie, Twinkie. Forgive me, but it all sounds the same to me. Anyway, Mrs. Duncan, I think I can safely rule you out as a murder suspect. I've been wrong once or twice in my life, but I'm willing to take a gamble. Or—to let you think I'm taking a gamble.'' Spangle grinned.

Jane Duncan laughed, but Dewey detected a twinge of disappointment in her friend's face. Jane, with the ebullience of the innocent, thought she might enjoy the thrill of being a real suspect. Dewey knew differently; she had seen how suspicion could cast its dark shadow over the most buoyant of natures. Jane was lucky the lieutenant could thus clear her name, using Dewey as her alibi. Dewey was aware that Spangle had inquired about her of the Hamilton police—her friend George Farnham had telephoned her with that interesting bit of news on Sunday. She must remember to thank the good Captain Fielding Booker when she got back home.

Spangle was going on. "But about the business of the faked-up painting, Mrs. Duncan. We are kind of at a loss. I was hoping you could shed some light on that issue for us.'' He withdrew a small notebook from the pocket of his jacket and flipped it open.

Jane Duncan's face brightened. "Certainly, Lieutenant.

Although"—her face clouded with doubt—"I don't know a blessed thing, really."

"Well, let's just see about that, ma'am. According to Lucas Hanover, the sale of the painting was approved by the Bently's board of trustees."

"Was it? I don't think so, Captain."

"Lieutenant, ma'am."

"Yes. No—I don't remember anything about it at a meeting. The first *whiff* I had of it was at the Bently dinner. Lucas Hanover was there, looking mighty pleased with himself, and it seemed to me that something was up. So I asked him what he was so happy about, and he gave me a hint. Naturally, I expressed my surprise."

"You recall no official trustee approval?"

"No. No—but of course, I have been a trustee for a comparatively brief time—three months, give or take. There might have been a decision made before that time."

"Perhaps." Spangle made a note. "But Hanover says the approval came through about a month ago."

"And who told him of this approval, Lieutenant?" asked Dewey James in a quiet voice.

"I believe it was the dead woman, Lainie Guiles."

"I see." Dewey pursed her lips. She was determined not to interfere.

"Something on your mind, Mrs. James?"

"Well, yes." She leaned forward, eager to talk. "Lieutenant, don't you consider it the *slightest* bit odd that nobody but this Mr. Hanover seemed to know that such a sale had been approved?"

"I do." He smiled. Amateurs. "Of course we have people looking into that, Mrs. James."

"I'm quite certain you do," said Dewey in her best placatory tones. "The thing is, Lieutenant, that someone at the Bently connived in the sale of that painting—real or forged."

"Yes, ma'am. That's pretty clear, on the evidence, although I appreciate your pointing it out to me."

"Oh, dear. Now I suppose you think me an interfering old lady from the boondocks, Lieutenant—"

"By no means, Mrs. James," said Spangle in empty protest. Dewey saw right through him.

"And I know for a fact that you have been in touch with my *dear* friend Fielding Booker."

"What's this?" asked Jane Duncan sharply. She scowled at Lieutenant Spangle. "You have been checking up on my houseguest, Captain?"

"Lieutenant. Yes, indeed, Mrs. Duncan. We've checked up on every blessed soul that has had any involvement whatsoever with the woman who was murdered. Surely you don't object."

"Of course I do! *Most* strenuously. I can vouch for Dewey James myself."

"No need, Mrs. Duncan." Spangle smiled. "In fact, as I've pointed out, we have relied on your friend here to vouch for you."

"It's quite all right, Jane," Dewey reassured her friend. "It's the way these things work. At least I've given you an alibi for the night that Lainie was killed. But, Lieutenant, there are one or two things I really think you ought to consider."

"Yes, ma'am?" Spangle had put away his notebook and risen from his chair. Clearly he thought there was nothing more that these women could offer him. He had got what he had come for—confirmation that the Bently trustees had never approved the sale of the painting. It had been cooked up between Hanover and Lainie Guiles, and now Lainie Guiles was dead.

"Yes. Forgive me, Jane," she said in a solemn voice. "Lieutenant—I think you must find out why Lainie Guiles took out a copy of Donald Brewster's play from the Dixon Library."

"What?" Jane Duncan exclaimed. "*The Latter-Day Don Juan*?"

"Bear with me, Jane," Dewey pleaded gently.

"Well, now, Mrs. James," said the lieutenant, "I can't say that I exactly follow your train of thought here. What's the play got to do with it?"

Dewey briefly described her visit to the Dixon Library, glossing over her ignorance of computers to come to the point. Lainie Guiles had checked out the library's copy of the script, which was a very odd circumstance, all things considered.

"Maybe she just wanted to *read* it, Dewey," Jane protested.

"And why not?" agreed Spangle.

"I think you should look for that play, Lieutenant. You will recall that Donald Brewster won the Bently Medallion for that play. It is deeply tied in to this matter. If the script wasn't among Lainie's effects, which I suspect it wasn't—"

"I can't say yes or no, Mrs. James," put in Spangle, obviously at a loss. In fact, there had been no copy of *The Latter-Day Don Juan* at Lainie's apartment. Nor in her office at the Bently Foundation. But then again—the police had not known they should be looking for it. He stared hard at Dewey James. What was this old bat up to, anyway?

"My suspicion is, Lieutenant, that the person who murdered Lainie Guiles has got it."

"Oh, I doubt that, Mrs. James. I think, you know, that it's just too great a coincidence, this business of the faked-up painting. Dollars to doughnuts our murderer is the one who tried to pass that painting off as the real McCoy."

"Lucas Hanover," said Jane softly.

"Oh? Do you think so?" Dewey shook her head. "I very much doubt it, Jane. Good heavens—the newscast told us that the forgery was destined to be discovered almost immediately. Anyone could have detected it."

"Not without replacing the frame," said Spangle. He wanted to rid himself of all doubt, to justify his assumptions. "Hanover counseled Richard Basson not to mess with the frame. Why would he do that if he wasn't worried that the forgery would be found out?"

"Oh, good heavens, Lieutenant," said Dewey. "Even in Hamilton we have heard of the fabled excesses of Richard Basson. Hanover probably thought that Basson would put some monstrous modern *thing* around the painting."

"Hmm."

"Lieutenant—I'll tell you what. You find the copy of Donald's play, and I'll talk to Lily Feldspar and find out why she lost her job. Then we'll compare notes. How's that?"

Francis Spangle saw an easy way out from this crazy conversation. "Fine, fine." He put on his coat, smiled, and said goodbye.

Jane turned on Dewey. "What was all that about Donald's play, Dewey? You don't think that Donald is involved in all this scandal, do you?"

"Jane, dear—" Dewey began.

"Donald has been behaving so *oddly*," Jane went on. "Oh, Dewey, I won't be able to bear it if there is something dreadfully wrong."

"Jane," said Dewey firmly, "there has been a murder. In my book, that is something dreadfully wrong. Obviously your policeman is barking up the wrong tree, but if he won't listen to reason, then it's up to us. It really is." She smiled at Jane. "I thought you wanted to help me be a detective?"

"I do. I did, that is. Now, I'm not so sure. You'll drag Donald down, and I'll never see him again."

"Hush, Jane dear. We'll get to the bottom of it." She looked at her watch. "Do you mind if I use your telephone?"

"Of course not. Who are you calling?"

"Never mind. What time is your meeting, Jane?"

"Oh, the Bently meeting. In half an hour. I wish I had never heard of the Bently Foundation."

"Do you? I think it's rather a nice little operation. Just needs housecleaning, like so many old establishments." She smiled an encouraging smile at her friend. "Jane, I suggest you get yourself ready for the meeting. I'll see you when it's over. We'll go somewhere nice for dinner. On me. How about a lively little jazz club or something, down in the Village? It's been years since I've gone jazzing.''

Jane assented. Then, looking more dispirited than Dewey had ever seen her, she headed up the stairs to change for the Bently meeting. When she was safely out of earshot, Dewey picked up the telephone and dialed the Department of English at Hencope College.

21

DEWEY'S TELEPHONE CALL to Andrea Follet was short but to the point. The professor agreed to meet Dewey at the Bently Mansion at three-thirty.

Dewey next put in a call to Donald Brewster, who answered the phone with a voice more sullen and despondent than Dewey might have thought possible.

"Donald? It's Dewey James calling."

"Ah. Hello, Dewey. Look, I'm terribly sorry about last night. I just wasn't feeling up to *Les Misérables*."

"Never mind about that, Donald. We didn't go after all." She lowered her voice to a whisper. "Don't tell Jane, but I can't stand Victor Hugo."

"You and me both," said Donald Brewster emphatically.

"Well, Donald, by now you have heard the latest news, no doubt."

"Can't avoid it," said Donald, his pleasing voice regaining some of its buoyancy.

"And poor, dear Jane is fit to be tied. She's got so many people telephoning, and the police have come here to question her yet again, and the whole thing is a perfect mess."

"The price of fame," said Donald with a laugh. "I know how she feels."

"Do you, now? Well, I am hoping that you'll do me a

small favor. Would you be good enough? I think it will help Jane so much through her present difficulties.''

"Whatever you say, Dewey dear."

Dewey sensed relief in Donald's voice, as though he were looking for a guiding light out of a dark and altogether Byzantine maze.

"Well." Dewey took a breath. "I have asked Andrea Follet to meet me at the Bently in forty-five minutes. There is going to be an emergency meeting of the trustees, and I think it would be best for all concerned, Donald, if you could come along."

Donald Brewster considered this suggestion in silence for a long moment. Dewey waited patiently. "All right," he said at last. "Although how you—"

"Thank you so very much, Donald." She hung up and sat, lost in thought for a moment. Then, steeling her nerve, she dialed the number of the 16th Precinct of the New York City Police Department.

"Lieutenant Spangle, please. This is Dewey James calling."

At the Bently Mansion Maria greeted Dewey eagerly.

"So far, *nothing*," said Maria as Dewey pulled off her coat. "Is that okay?"

"I think it's far better that way, my dear. Is Mr. Fenhaden in his office?"

"Yeah. He's been sulking all afternoon."

"I think he's been sulking all his life," Dewey responded.

"Too true," Maria agreed. "What next, Dewey?"

"Well, my dear, I have a little plan. I've invited a few people to join the trustees meeting. Are the trustees here?"

"Just Mrs. Duncan, Mr. Montrose, and Mr. Philpotts. You know, the department store guy."

"Oh! Benjamin Philpotts?" Dewey looked surprised. "I had no idea he was still alive."

"He's about a hundred and two, I think," said Maria with

a twinkle. "But he's a game old guy. Never misses a meeting."

"How's his hearing?"

"He wears one of those things in his ear, but I guess it's okay. He always stops to talk to me, and I've never noticed a problem."

"Good," said Dewey with a quick glance at her watch. "Because if Lieutenant Spangle doesn't get here soon, we may need an objective witness. Is Marge Gantry in?"

Maria nodded. "She didn't even stop to say hello, though. She looks terrible."

"I'll bet she does. Well, it will all soon be over with, my dear. Then you can go on to fame and fortune in the theater."

"Right. Get away from the crackpots, you mean? I think it might be worse, working full-time in the theater."

"You may have a point. By the way, Maria, have you heard anything from Mr. Lippincott lately?"

"No. I feel so sorry for him, Mrs. James. He's such a nice man."

"Is he?"

"Yep. Lainie Guiles broke his heart, I think."

"Perhaps. But you know it takes two to break a heart, Maria." Dewey looked about her abstractedly. "I think I'll go upstairs for a little chat with Marge. Would you hold down the fort for me?"

"Sure thing."

Dewey headed up the carpeted stairs once more to Marge Gantry's domain. She was instantly aware, when she entered the gallery, of the empty space on the wall where the Chatard painting had hung. She went on past it and knocked at the half-open door of Marge's office.

"Oh. Mrs. James," said Marge dully.

"Hello, Mrs. Gantry," said Dewey brightly. "I was hoping you could spare me a minute or two. Would that be all right?"

"What for?"

"Good heavens, I am certain you know why I have come."

Marge eyed Dewey warily. "No."

"About the painting, of course." Dewey sat herself down in a small armchair opposite Marge Gantry's desk. It was the same chair that Lainie Guiles had sat in, two days before her murder. "I don't think your little idea will work, you see. And before things get too far out of hand, I thought you might like to unburden yourself."

"I have no idea what you're talking about," Marge said unconvincingly. "I have suffered a terrible loss here—"

"*Au contraire*," said Dewey brightly. "You have, in fact, preserved your precious painting from loss. Haven't you, Marge?"

"What?"

"I can imagine that it was actually rather easy for you. That annual report that you were preparing, the first time I came through. You were using a photograph of the Chatard painting in that, weren't you?"

"That's right."

"Well, then. It was all as simple as pie. All you needed to do was to send the *real* painting off to be photographed, and replace it with a forgery when it came back. Easy."

"That's absurd. Why would I do that?"

"Well, I have to admit that if I were in your shoes, I would have been tempted to do the same thing. Terry Fenhaden had found out about the sale of the painting—and he had found out, in fact, that Lucas Hanover was planning to sell it to none other than Richard Basson. Who is, if you don't mind my saying it, the embodiment of crass modern commercialism."

"You're right about that, at least," replied Marge Gantry.

"Yes. You couldn't abide the idea that someone so—so *unformed* should possess a part of your fabulous collection. A substitution was a simple thing. And by making such an obvious forgery, you ensured that no one would ever be tempted to split up the Bently Collection in the future.

Where would the Bently find a buyer, after such a scandal?''

"I think you've said enough, Mrs. James." There was a dangerous glint in Marge Gantry's eye.

"Perhaps. But a word to the wise, my dear. That's all. It's one thing to protect your precious collection, and quite another to let Lucas Hanover's career go down the drain. He's not a bad man, after all."

Marge Gantry stared at Dewey for a long moment. Then she nodded, slowly, and quietly began to cry.

"I wouldn't take it to heart, Mrs. Gantry," Dewey said. "Only make amends, if you can."

"Make amends for what?" said a voice. Turning round in her chair, Dewey saw that Lieutenant Spangle had arrived.

"Oh! So glad you could come, Lieutenant. You know Mrs. Gantry, I believe." She rose quickly and took the policeman by the elbow. "But our business here today has nothing to do with Marge and her collection." She hustled him out of the office, leaving Marge to preside alone over her precious domain.

"What was all that about?" Spangle protested as Dewey hurried him down the stairs.

"Nothing. Nothing at all. You're needed in the dining room, Lieutenant. But wait here, just a moment, won't you?"

Dewey stuck her head into Maria's office. "Anyone here?"

"Andrea Follet is here!" Maria exclaimed. "I put her in Terry's old office, along with Mr. Brewster."

"Ah," said Dewey. "Lieutenant, I think it's time you arrested your murderer. Shall we join the trustees? Maria, get Terry and the two others, would you? Have everyone join us in the dining room."

Lieutenant Spangle, his face a mask of impatient confusion, gave Dewey a long, hard look. "This," he said in a firm voice, "had better be good. Damn good."

"Follow me, if you please, Lieutenant."

* * *

"These goings-on," Lawrence Montrose was saying, "have naturally brought us all to a point where it is imperative that we marshal our resources—"

"Excuse us, everyone," said Dewey as she and Lieutenant Spangle burst into the room. "Mr. Montrose. I hope you will forgive this intrusion. But I thought it much the simplest way to clear things up. You don't mind, do you, if Lieutenant Spangle and I interrupt for a moment?"

Lawrence Montrose scowled at Dewey. "Not at all, Mrs. James," he said, his voice full of sarcasm. "We always invite policemen and strangers to our meetings."

"Well, I'm hardly a stranger," contradicted Dewey. "I'm Jane Duncan's best friend." She turned as Andrea Follet and Donald Brewster entered the room, followed by Maria Porter and Terry Fenhaden. "The rest of the group, of course, you know."

Montrose didn't struggle. "Fine, fine. Everyone have a seat. Now, as I was saying, we must marshal our resources—"

"Excuse me once more, Mr. Montrose," said Dewey pointedly. "If you don't mind, I'd like a chance to tell you all why we are here."

"Has something to do with all this funny business," said Benjamin Philpotts, his aged cheeks flapping with the exertion of speech. "Got a policeman there, haven't you?"

"No flies on him," muttered Terry Fenhaden. Dewey fixed him with a look.

"Yes, indeed, Mr. Philpotts. It has something to do with all this funny business." She looked at Andrea Follet and then at Donald Brewster. "Donald, would you care to begin?"

"Yes, indeed." He glanced toward Jane, and then began to address the assembled group. "Andrea Follet, as you may or may not know, is a member of the Pinkie Selection Committee."

Andrea Follet acknowledged this fact with a small nod, and Brewster went on.

"On the night of the Pinkie Dinner, when the official announcement of my selection was to be made, she paid me a visit. Over cocktails in my apartment, she described to me a situation which, I can only say, was galling in the extreme. She claimed that one of her graduate students had discovered a play, written in the early part of this century, to which my latest effort, *The Latter-Day Don Juan*, bore a striking resemblance. So she said."

"Is this true, Andrea?" asked Terry Fenhaden.

Andrea Follet ignored the question, and Brewster resumed. "It struck me at the time as a most remarkable coincidence of timing. Here I was, about to be lauded by a distinguished institution, for something I had written. And here was one member of the innermost circle of that institution coming to me not to congratulate me, but to—to what, Andrea?"

"To tell you what I knew," she said simply.

"Ah. To tell me what she knew. Which was that I had 'borrowed' material from an unknown writer and translated it into a personal success of great magnitude."

"Had you?" asked Spangle with a reluctant look in Dewey's direction.

"No. No, indeed. But the circumstances, you see, were rather awkward."

"Why?" asked Jane Duncan.

"Because it was true that this other play existed. It wasn't really at all like mine; it had been written, in the first place, for an entirely different period. *The Latter-Day Don Juan* is quite modern, whereas this play by Margaret Leslie, called *The Runabout*, was really a Victorian melodrama. But there it was—a most uncomfortable coincidence."

"Ms. Follet," said Spangle, "you had better tell us what you had in mind."

"All I had in mind," said Andrea Follet, her discomfort evident, "was to let Donald know what was being said."

"What purpose would that serve?"

"Merely to apprise him of it," she said, all conviction draining from her voice.

"Not to extort money from him in exchange for your silence?"

A hush fell on the room. It was Dewey James who had uttered the question on everyone's mind. "Isn't it true, Ms. Follet, that the Pinkie Selection Committee has made a practice, in years past, of extorting a portion of the prize money from the people who win the Medallion?"

"That's absurd," said Lawrence Montrose.

"Is it? I wonder." She turned to Maria. "Maria, would you kindly get Mr. Garrett Brown on the telephone for us?"

"Sure thing, Dewey," said Maria, bouncing up out of her chair to comply.

"Wait a minute, Maria," said Montrose. "In case you are unaware of this fact, Mrs. James, Maria works for the Bently Foundation. I'll not have outsiders giving her orders."

"Very well," responded Dewey, her face a picture of serenity.

"Go on, girl," growled Benjamin Philpotts. "You be quiet, Montrose. Go on, Maria, do what the lady asks. This whole situation, frankly, stinks." He looked disgusted.

"That won't be necessary," said Andrea Follet. She had regained some of her composure, and now she turned on Montrose with a furious look. "You!"

"What on earth—"

"You were the one who insisted that your girlfriend be promoted to director. Look where it got us, Lawrence. Well, I'm not going to stand for it any longer."

"Girlfriend?" asked Philpotts in a querulous voice. "Lainie Guiles was your girlfriend? I thought she ran with that actor fellow."

"Oh, shut up," said Montrose.

"It's true, Lieutenant," said Andrea Follet. Evidently she

had decided to speak her mind. "I don't know how Mrs. James found out about it—"

"At the library," said Dewey simply.

Andrea Follet chuckled. "She went to the library. Isn't that nice? Well, it's true, Mrs. James, that we had something going. It wasn't so bad, really—a small payback."

"Kickback, you mean," said Spangle.

"Whatever." She glowered at Donald Brewster. "But Donald didn't care to play. By the time I got to talk to him about things, I think he must have somehow been tipped off."

"She's lying," said Montrose. "That woman is lying, I tell you. And Lainie Guiles was a first-class—"

"Now, *you* shut up," said Philpotts. "Go on, woman."

"Well, that's it, really." Andrea Follet opened her eyes wide. "I know it wasn't right, exactly, but it didn't seem to do anyone any harm. A little present for the Pinkie Selectors. That's all it amounted to."

"Blackmail and extortion," said Spangle fiercely, "is what it amounted to."

"Like hell it did. You just try to prove a word of it. I'll have you up for slander, Follet."

Terry Fenhaden had been so uncharacteristically silent throughout the proceedings that everyone had nearly forgotten him. Now he spoke.

"No wonder Donald was so rude to me," he said. "I only wanted to—"

"Terry, now it's your turn to shut up," said Donald. "I don't know what you wanted from me when you called, but if I were you, I would be very careful about talking. Especially now."

"Mr. Montrose," said Dewey firmly. "Have you got anything to add to Ms. Follet's statement?"

Lawrence Montrose glowered at Dewey, and the tip of his snub nose seemed to quiver.

"Such as," Dewey went on, "what happened after the Pinkie Dinner—when you arrived at Lainie's apartment?"

"Oh, no, you don't," said Montrose. "Don't start with me, lady, or you'll regret it."

"Well, honestly, Mr. Montrose. You don't think that Lainie Guiles was foolish enough to uncover your little scheme without making sure she had evidence, do you?"

"What evidence?"

"Why, Mr. Brown, of course. Garrett Brown—the muckraking writer for the *Clarion Call*. I imagine he has the whole story, or nearly. What are you going to do about that? Kill him as well?"

With a sudden burst of ferocity, Lawrence Montrose leapt from his seat. Before anyone in the room could respond, he had Dewey James in a stranglehold. It took the combined strength of Lieutenant Spangle and Donald Brewster to bring him down. When Montrose had been subdued, Spangle put handcuffs on him.

"Assault, anyway, Montrose. With deadly intent. That should be good enough to start with."

22

WHEN THE FIREWORKS at the Bently were over, and Andrea Follet and Lawrence Montrose had been taken away by Lieutenant Spangle, Jane Duncan had invited everyone to come around for a drink. She had even gone upstairs to ask Marge Gantry, but she found the collection door locked.

All but Fenhaden had accepted Jane's invitation; everyone had felt, very keenly, the need of a drink. Benjamin Philpotts had even consented to come along; and Sandra Gossage, Jane's housekeeper, was thoroughly put out when Jane insisted upon heating up some hors d'oeuvres in the kitchen.

"Well!" exclaimed Dewey James. "Now, I suppose, we can get on with the business of getting the two of you married to each other."

"Married? These two are getting married?" Benjamin Philpotts asked loudly. "Why didn't you tell me, Jane?" He rose slowly from his seat and shuffled across the rug to plant a wet kiss on her cheek. Maria giggled, and Jane laughed.

"It's not a secret, Benjamin. That is—not any longer."

"Many thanks to you, Dewey." Donald Brewster looked at her thoughtfully. "I don't know how you figured it out—"

"It was just luck, really. The Susan Dixon Library has the most fascinating computer system. I had a long talk with the man there, and I think I might like to have the same kind of thing in Hamilton.''

''Wait a minute, Dewey. You mean you figured it all out at the library?''

''Well, yes. You see, Lainie Guiles had been doing research on the Medallion winners. Which I thought was *most* odd, considering that she had been working at the Bently for ten years. It made me wonder. And then Lily Feldspar had lost her job, and Garrett Brown was trying to do a story on the foundation—and it seemed to me quite natural that there was something fishy going on.''

''Exactly,'' seconded Jane Duncan. ''That's *exactly* how we reasoned it, Donald.''

Dewey smiled. ''And since everything else was so above-board, it had to be that silly secret committee, up to no good. And when I learned that there was prize money, well, then, naturally I saw that it would be a perfect way to extort a little cash. I don't know what Lainie Guiles had in mind—perhaps she merely wanted a slice of the pie; or perhaps she meant to expose Montrose. We'll probably never know.''

''Poor Hayden,'' said Donald Brewster.

''He'll be fine,'' said Jane. ''He'll be much better without her around. You watch.''

''Was everyone in on it? The whole committee, I mean?'' asked Maria.

''All but Sophia Fuller, I would imagine,'' said Dewey. ''She didn't seem the blackmailing type to me.''

''I wonder what kind of evidence Lieutenant Spangle will find,'' said Brewster.

''That play, for one thing. Which Lainie had only taken out of the library the day of the Pinkie Dinner.''

''Oh!'' said Maria. ''That must be why he kept trying to sneak in there. He was trying to get rid of the evidence!''

''That's right. Didn't you tell me, Maria, that he had asked Fenhaden to clear out?''

''Yup.'' Maria nodded vigorously, her dark eyes shining.

"But Terry wouldn't do it. And he locked the door every time he left the office."

"Lucky for us he did," said Dewey. "Well, now—how about a toast to the bride and groom?"

"How about," said Donald Brewster, "a toast to our maid of honor and sleuth extraordinaire?" He raised his glass to Dewey, who blushed becomingly—but she was well pleased.

On Friday at lunchtime Dewey James—resplendent in her new dress from Bergdorf's—served yet again as Jane Duncan's maid of honor. Hayden Lippincott, still looking much the worse for wear, was Donald Brewster's best man. While the couple recited their vows, Dewey held Jane's bouquet and thought quietly to herself about her late husband, Brendan.

The marriage ceremony took three or four minutes; and when it was over, the four of them piled into a waiting limousine and headed for a waterfront restaurant in Brooklyn. There they tucked in to an extraordinary feast of champagne and lobster and were very merry.

"Well, now, Dewey—what do you think?" Jane held out her ring finger for Dewey to admire. Donald had presented her with a remarkably beautiful star sapphire, a family heirloom.

"Simply gorgeous, Jane," said Dewey warmly.

"Dewey—what about that nice man who's so in love with you?"

"I have no idea who you mean, Jane," Dewey lied.

"The one who cooks so well. You're a disaster in the kitchen, Dewey—the only person who's worse is my cook, Sandra."

"I do all right," Dewey protested.

"You could do better." She smiled at Donald and kissed his cheek. "Right, old friend?"

"Yes, indeed, my dear."

Dewey James looked at them; and suddenly she wanted very much to go home to Hamilton.